DRAW SCIENCE

REPTILES AND AMPHIBIANS

By Nina Kidd

LOWELL HOUSE JUVENILE

LOS ANGELES

CONTEMPORARY BOOKS

CHICAGO

Copyright © 1998 by RGA Publishing Group, Inc.
All rights reserved. No part of this work may be reproduced or transmitted in any form or by any means, electronic or mechanical, including photocopying and recording, or by any information storage or retrieval system, except as may be expressly permitted by the 1976 Copyright Act or in writing by the publisher.

Publisher: Jack Artenstein
Director of Publishing Services: Rena Copperman
Editorial Director: Brenda Pope-Ostrow
Director of Juvenile Development: Amy Downing
Typesetter: Treesha Runnells

Lowell House books can be purchased at special discounts when ordered in bulk for premiums and special sales. Contact Department TC at the following address:
Lowell House Juvenile
2020 Avenue of the Stars, Suite 300
Los Angeles, CA 90067

Manufactured in the United States of America

Library of Congress Catalog Card Number: 97-76091

ISBN: 1-56565-936-8

10 9 8 7 6 5 4 3 2 1

Contents

Getting Started 4
What You'll Need 4
Finishing Your Drawing 6
The Indopacific Crocodile 8
The Gharial 10
The Marine Iguana 12
The Gila Monster 14
The Komodo Dragon 16
The Boa Constrictor 18
The Australian Frilled Lizard 20
The Jackson's Chameleon 22
The American Chameleon 24
The Giant Land Tortoise 26
The Warty Newt 28
The Gulf Coast Toad 30
The South American Pygmy Marsupial Frog 32
The Chinese Spiny Newt 34
The Texas Horned Lizard 36
Boulanger's Arrow Poison Frog 38
The Surinam Toad 40
The American Bullfrog 42
The Green Sea Turtle 44
The Northern Fence Lizard 46
The American Alligator 48
The Ornate Box Turtle 50
The Tuatara 52
The Western Diamondback Rattlesnake 54
Backgrounds 57
Bringing Your Animal to Life 58
Making Your Animal Seem Larger (or Smaller) 60
Tips on Color 62
Glossary 64

Getting Started

This book shows you how to draw 24 different reptiles and amphibians. There are lots of different ways to draw, and here are just a few. You'll find some helpful hints throughout this book to help make your drawings the best they can be.

Before you begin, here are some tips that every aspiring artist should know!

- Use a large sheet of paper and make your drawing fill up the space. That way, it's easy to see what you are doing, and it will give you plenty of room to add details.

- When you are blocking in large shapes, draw by moving your whole arm, not just your fingers or your wrist.

- Experiment with different kinds of lines: Do a light line, then gradually bear down for a wider and darker one. You'll find that just by changing the thickness of a line, your whole picture will look different! Also, try groups of lines, drawing all the lines in a group straight, crossing, curved, or jagged.

- Remember that every artist has his or her own style. That's why the pictures you draw won't look exactly like the ones in the book. Instead, they'll reflect your own creative touch.

- Most of all, have fun!

What You'll Need

PAPER
Many kinds of paper can be used for drawing, but some are better than others. For pencil drawing, avoid newsprint or rough paper because they don't erase well. Instead, use a large pad of bond paper (or a similar type). The paper doesn't have to be thick, but it should be uncoated, smooth, and cold pressed. You can find bond paper at an art store. If you are using ink, a dull-finished, coated paper works well.

PENCILS, CHARCOAL, AND PENS
A regular school pencil is fine for the drawings in this book, but try to use one with a soft lead. Pencils with a soft lead are labeled #2; #3 pencils have a hard lead. If you want a thicker lead, ask an art store clerk or your art teacher for an artist's drafting pencil.

Charcoal works well when you want a very black line, so if you're just starting to draw with charcoal, use a charcoal pencil of medium to hard grade. You will be able to rub in shadows, then erase certain areas to make highlights. Work with large pieces of paper, as charcoal is difficult to control in small drawings. And remember that charcoal smudges easily!

If you want a smooth, thin ink line, try a rolling-point or a fiber-point pen. Art stores and bigger stationery stores have them in a variety of line widths and fun, bright colors.

ERASERS

An eraser is one of your most important tools! Besides removing unwanted lines and cleaning up smudges, erasers can be used to make highlights and textures. Get a soft plastic type (the white ones are good), or for very small areas, a gray kneaded eraser can be helpful. Don't take off ink with an eraser because it will ruin the drawing paper. If you must take an ink line out of your picture, use liquid whiteout.

OTHER HANDY TOOLS

Facial tissues are helpful for creating soft shadows—just go over your pencil marks with a tissue, gently rubbing the area you want smoothed out.

A square of metal window screen is another tool that can be used to make shadows. Hold it just above your paper and rub a soft pencil lead across it. Then rub the shavings from the pencil into the paper to make a smooth shadowed area in your picture. If you like, you can sharpen the edge of the shadow with your eraser.

You also will need a pencil sharpener, but if you don't have one, rub a small piece of sandpaper against the side of your pencil to keep the point sharp.

Finishing Your Drawing

As you'll see from the animals in this book, different skins and shells have different textures. You can use special drawing methods to make them look three-dimensional and natural. Try some of the techniques demonstrated below.

HATCHING

Hatching is a group of short, straight lines used to create a texture or a shadow. The hatching either can show that the surface is flat, using straight lines, or how rounded it is, depending on the amount of curve in the lines.

This horned lizard's scales—its hardened sections of skin—are prickly and stick up unevenly. Suggest each prickly scale by making quick, short pencil strokes in one direction. Arrange the darkest strokes to create circular patterns. As the tone fades toward the center of each pattern, use lighter strokes. Leave white spaces between the markings, and make the spine points sharp and dark.

CONTOUR DRAWING

Many turtles, such as this ornate box turtle, have very visible "growth plates" on their shells. The ridges that appear around each plate can be wider or narrower, depending on how much food was available that year. Show that the plates are curved and the ridges are bumpy by making the ridge outlines thick and dark on the lower edges and lighter along the upper edges.

TEXTURE DRAWING

Look at the gharial to see another way to finish a drawing. The network of creases on a crocodilian's skin is very much like a crumpled fishnet. Where the skin squeezes together around the base of a leg, the spaces between the creases get compressed and may be nearly triangular. On the broad sides of the body, the spaces can be almost rectangular. Be sure to make the lines wiggly, or your gharial will look like a checkerboard!

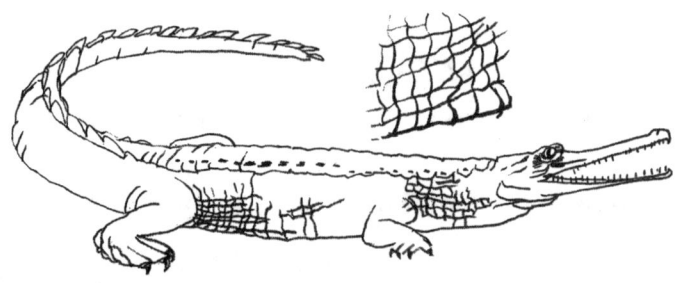

SMOOTH TONE

By using the side of your pencil, you can create a smooth texture on your creature. Starting with the areas you want to be light, stroke the paper very lightly and evenly. Put a little bit more pressure on your pencil as you move to the areas you want to be darker. If you want an area even smoother, go back and rub the pencil with a facial tissue, but rub gently! If you get smudges in areas you want to stay white, simply remove them with an eraser. Try this smooth texture on the horns or spines of the tuatara.

Another example of the smooth tone is shown on this Boulanger's arrow poison frog. Not only are amphibians sometimes boldly marked, they also must keep their skins wet. You can show the wet shine on its skin by leaving streaks of white on the bulges of its body and legs. At the lower edge of each streak, draw a dark edge, sharp against the white but fading below. Look closely at a shiny dark bottle or a dark car's hood to see how these light streaks take on the shape or the surface and make it look glossy.

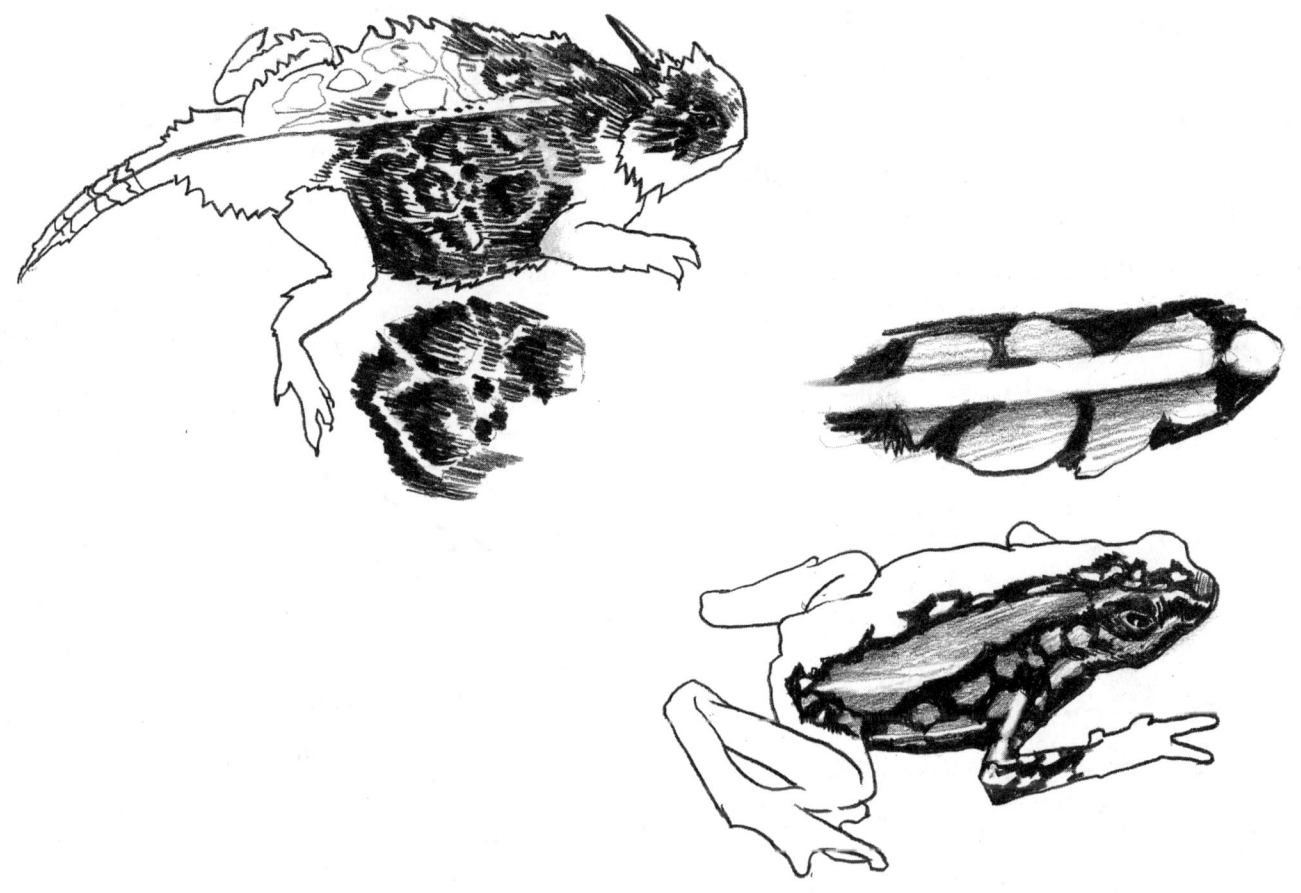

Now that you're armed with the basic drawing tools and techniques, you're ready to get started on the creatures in this book. What's more, you'll learn as you draw! After each drawing step, you'll find some scientific information that not only is fun and interesting to know, but also useful when it comes to drawing.

Throughout this book you'll find special drawing tips that will aid your progress. At the back of the book, extra techniques and hints for using color, casting shadows, and placing animals in a scene show you how to make the most of your drawings.

The Indopacific Crocodile lives in southeast Asia, anywhere from China and India south into the northern

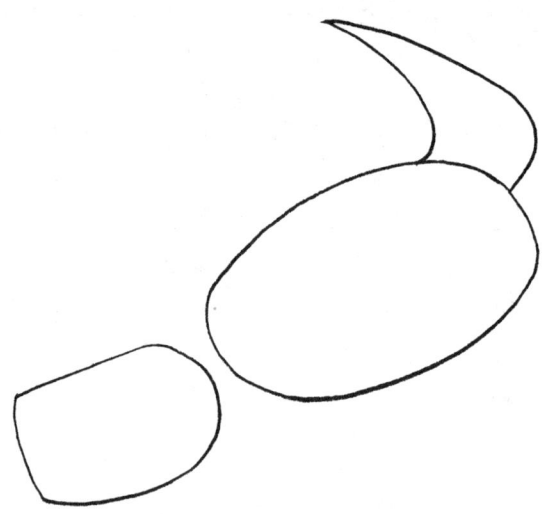

① Draw an oval for the body, adding a tail shape that tapers to a sharp tip. Create a small oval with a blunt end on the left side, but leave a gap for the neck.

Crocodiles have been on earth for millions of years and some lived alongside the dinosaurs. This species can grow longer than two automobiles end to end and weigh more than 2,200 pounds (990 kilograms)!

② Draw a *V* within the head shape. Connect the head to the body, and add the first joint of the foreleg and an outline of the hind leg.

The crocodile waits underwater until its prey is close, then it lunges on its short legs to grab the animal in its jaws.

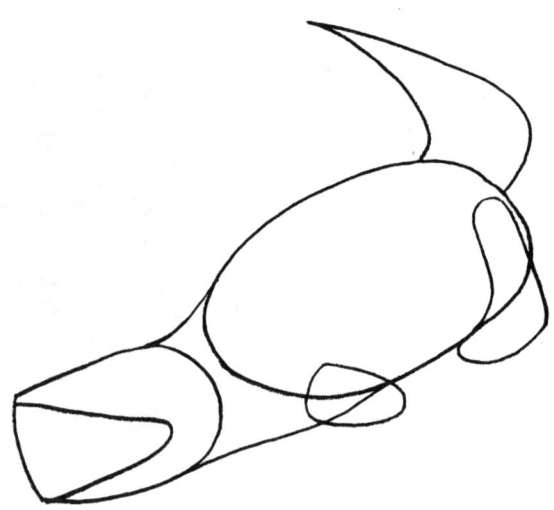

③ Add the lower edges of the tail on both the left and right sides of the original pointed shape. Then draw in the oval lower leg shape on the animal's left foreleg, and rounded shapes for legs on the far side of the body.

Longer than it is wide, the tail moves the animal forward in the water by sweeping it in S-shaped movements.

part of Australia. A carnivore, the Indopacific crocodile is responsible for nearly all crocodile attacks on humans where it is found.

---

④ Add the two forefeet and the eye, then shape the top of the tapered snout. Begin to detail its mouth. On its back, make six slightly curving lines that will mark the divisions between the rows of scales. Draw four lines on its tail, and sketch in petal shapes within the top curving edges of the tail.

The thick skin is protected by nonoverlapping scales called scutes. On the back, squarish bony plates embedded in the skin form an armor.

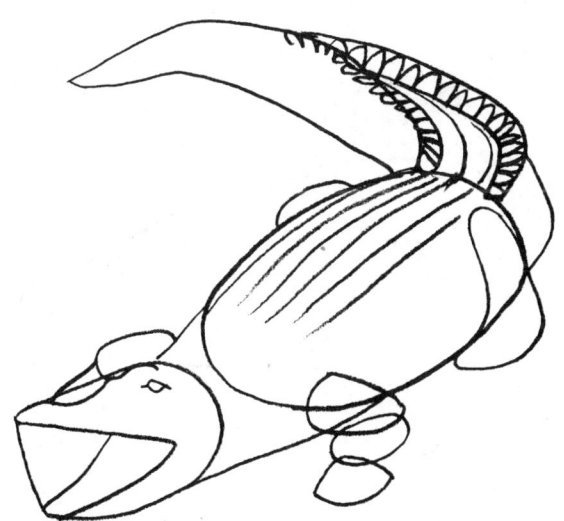

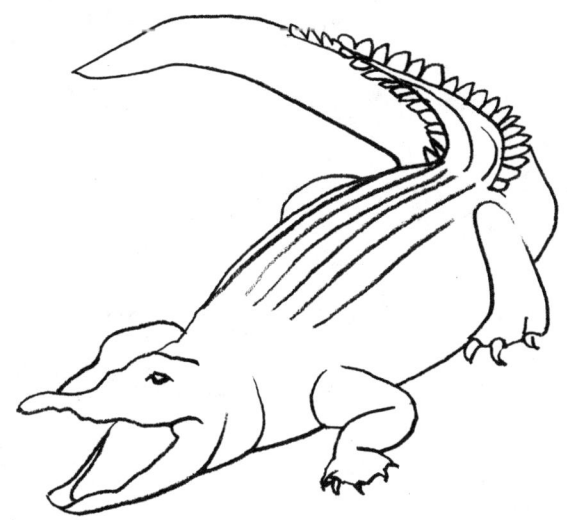

⑤ Draw the visible curved claws on the front and hind feet. Create the irregular inner edge of the upper and lower jaw, as well as the crease in the neck. Erase unneeded lines.

The jaws are designed for grabbing and holding prey, not chewing. Once the prey is quiet, the croc either shakes it apart or swallows it whole by tossing its own head back and letting the prey drop into its throat.

⑥ Add the triangle-shaped teeth, and shade inside the mouth. Draw curving crosswise lines on its back, and show the creases in the skin with wavy crisscross lines on its neck and legs. Further detail the head, and draw vertical lines on the tail. The younger animals especially have darker patches on their legs, belly, and tail. For a simple ground, draw horizontal lines underneath the crocodile.

When a croc loses a tooth, another replaces it as long as the animal is healthy. The mouth of a crocodile leaks because it doesn't have lips. Scientists think that crocodiles leave their mouths open to cool themselves as the moisture on the inside skin evaporates.

The Gharial is known as the fish-eating crocodile. While fossil remains of these animals have been found in North and South

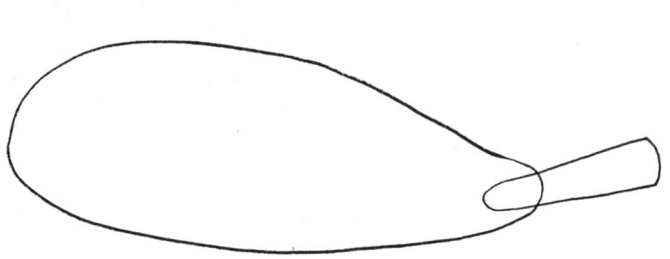

① Start with a long pear shape on its side. At the smaller end, draw a slender cone for the head and open jaws.

The gharial can grow to over 20 feet (6.2 meters) long. It lives in rivers where many people bathe and fish, but despite its threatening size, it has never been known to attack people.

② Draw a curving line within the pear shape to make a tapering body, and a smaller *V* within the cone for the jaws.

The tail, where extra fat is stored, is nearly as big around as the body. If necessary, a large animal can go for up to two years without a meal.

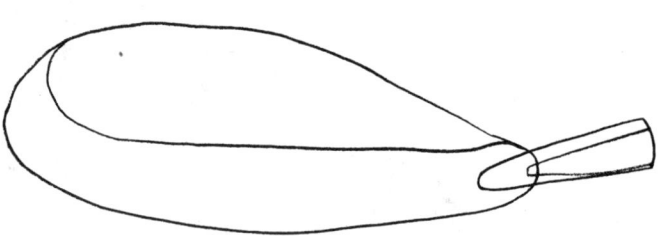

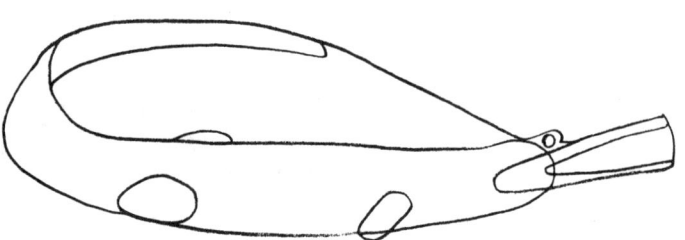

③ Draw ovals for the upper legs as shown. The round eye is in a bump above the jaws. Add the lower edge of the tail, which curves back behind the body.

Most of the gharial's food is fish, which it catches with quick sideways swipes of the head. The acid in its stomach is so strong, it can dissolve hair, bones, and even teeth!

America, as well as Africa and Asia, the only remaining species lives in the northern part of India.

④ Make a line along the body that will be the near edge of its back, turning into the top of the jagged tail. Add the ovals for the lower legs, and the curving edge of the inside of the mouth.

Raccoons and people prey on gharial eggs, and while the gharial is protected by law in India, it is still in danger of extinction.

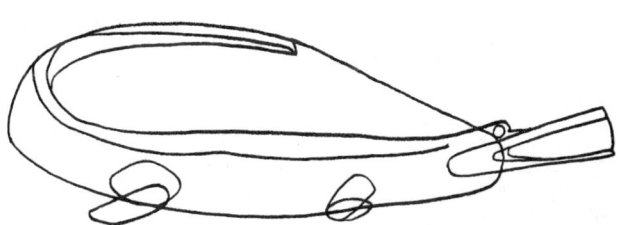

⑤ Add the hind foot and forefoot. Draw in a tail-fin ridge with fin shapes pointing toward the tail tip. Finish the ridge behind the eye, and erase any unneeded lines.

The name gharial *comes from the Hindi word* ghara, *which means "mud pot" and refers to a knob made of cartilage on the male animal's snout. As the knob grows, it creates a lid over the nostrils. When the male sniffs, he can make a buzzing sound, which he does when trying to attract a mate.*

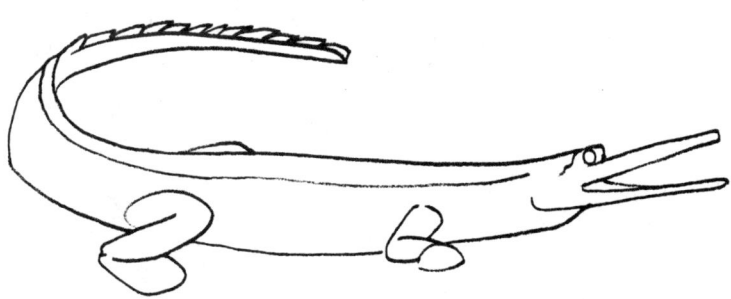

⑥ Finish by adding toes and claws and continuing the rows of tail fins. The gharial's head is relatively smooth surfaced, and its interlocking teeth are small and sharp, well adapted for holding slippery, wriggling fish. As you draw the crisscross pattern of the skin, the scales should be nearly white with darker speckles, and the dark lines between them should be well defined.

The female buries her eggs and stays near them, until she hears the babies' faint grunts. She then digs up the nest and helps the young break out of their eggs. Baby gharials live on insects, then tadpoles, frogs, and small fish.

The Marine Iguana is the only iguana we know of that eats only undersea plants. It is found only on the Galápagos Islands, part of the South

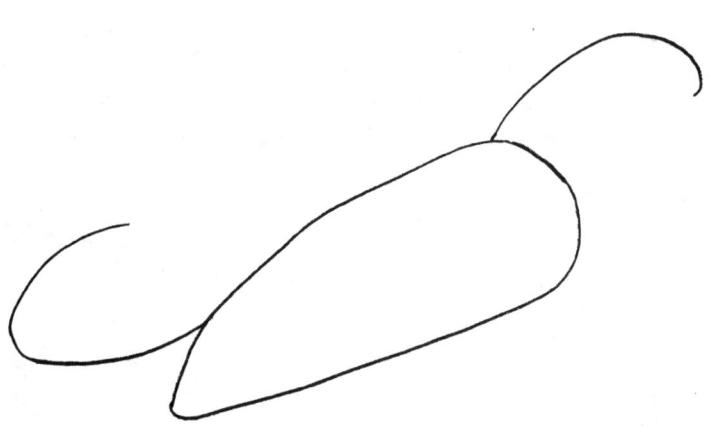

① Start with a long seed shape, broad at the upper end and narrow at the lower end. At the top corner, draw a down-curving loop for the neck and head. Near the lowest end, make another loop, slightly larger than the first and curving upward.

Marine iguanas dive more than 40 feet (12.4 meters) deep to find algae, kelp, and other undersea plants.

② Finish the head loop with an oval, and add two bent ovals for the upper legs. Add the lower edges of the tail, tapering to a point.

During the breeding season, the males fight fiercely, raising their toothy crests and lashing out with teeth and claws. Usually the animals don't hurt each other, but the smaller or weaker males leave the territory.

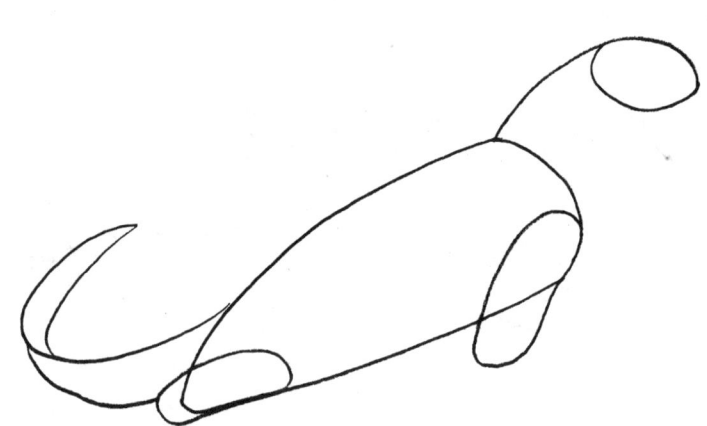

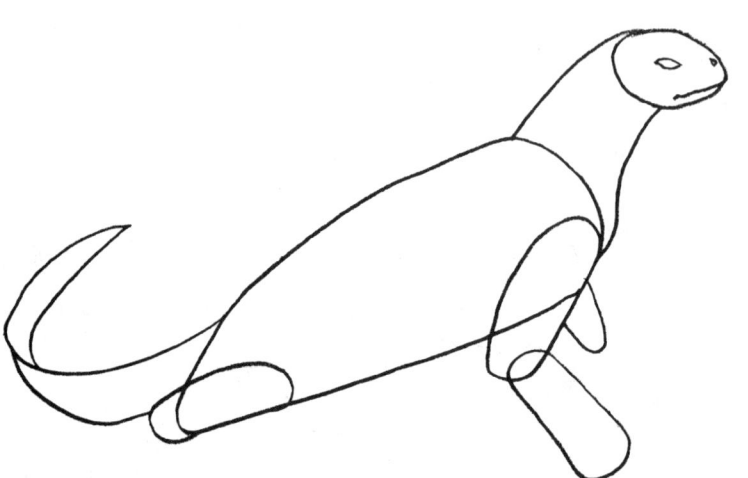

③ Complete the broad neck. Add the eye opening, mouth, and nostril. Suggest the lower forelegs.

Because the iguana depends on the temperature of its environment to avoid getting too cold or too hot, these animals bask on the sunny rocks of their island home to get warm before they dive into the cooler ocean.

American country of Ecuador. Other types of iguanas live on the ground and in trees. They eat insects and plants.

④ Repeat the line of the upper edge of the tail just above the first one to form a guideline for the crest. Above the back and head, the guideline should be wavy for the spinal crest. Below the chin, add another line for loose skin. Draw the broad shapes for the right feet and an oval for the left front foot.

Unlike marine iguanas, very few lizards eat only plants, and fewer still swim. Marine iguanas use their tall, flat tails and webbed toes to help them swim.

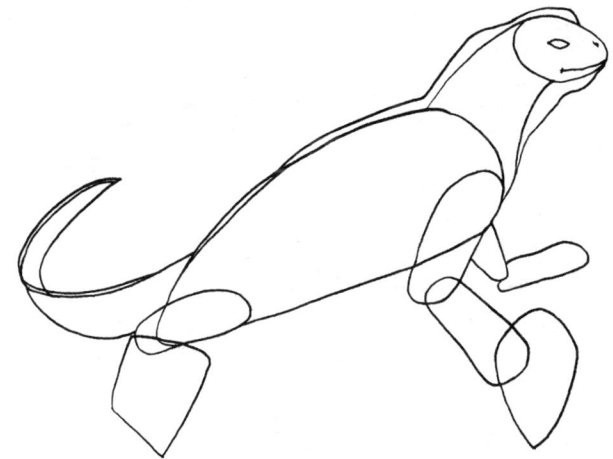

⑤ Draw in the eyeball and creases on the neck and around the legs. Inside the foot shapes, draw the long toes and heavy claws. Short backward-pointing lines along the tail are the spikes that may protect the tail from predators' bites. Erase any unneeded lines.

Baby iguanas often come out of the nest hole together. This way they can warn each other of a diving seabird. If they scatter, they may confuse the enemy and give themselves a better chance to escape.

⑥ Use a light crosshatching technique to shade under the iguana's body and on the lower sides of the legs, head, and tail. The wrinkly skin has a beady, fine scale—outline its irregular pebbly shapes. Darken the eye, claws, and the lower edges of the crest spikes.

Iguanas are endangered by humans, who either hunt them for their flesh or eggs, or destroy their habitat. The Galápagos marine iguana is protected by law, and the number of people visiting their islands is strictly controlled.

The Gila Monster
named after the river in Arizona where it was first described, is the only poisonous lizard

① Draw a large, curved rectangle shape and a smaller one, angled up away from the larger.

The adult lizard is just over 12 inches (30 centimeters) long and lives on birds' eggs.

② Add slightly elongated ovals for the upper foreleg and the hind end, which forms the upper hind legs.

The Gila monster is most active at night. If provoked, it will snap like an angry dog.

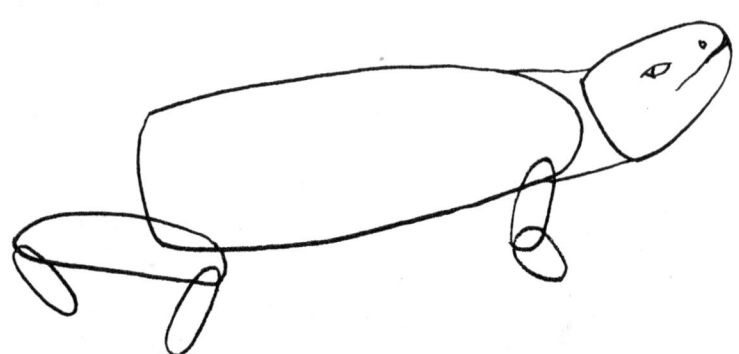

③ Connect the head and body, and draw ovals for the lower legs. Add the eye, nostril, and mouth.

Because of its unusual appearance and bright-colored beadlike scales, zoo owners and others trapped this animal for display. However, fearing it would be trapped into extinction, every state where it lives has placed the lizard on its list of protected wildlife.

living in the United States. When biting, it holds on tightly while poison in its mouth seeps into the bite wound.

---

④ Add ovals for the three visible feet and a thick S shape for the tail.

This lizard stores fat in its tail, which is normally thick and round. A thin tail means the animal has had to go without food for some time.

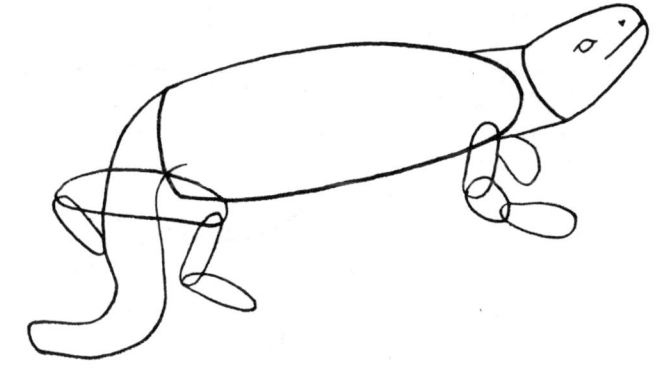

⑤ Draw in the toes, claws, and lower jaw. Smooth the joints of the legs, and begin to form the lines on the tail. Erase unneeded lines.

Though it moves slowly, the Gila monster has been known to climb low trees in search of eggs, which are its favorite food.

⑥ Now that you have your Gila monster drawn, it's time to shade its body. Color in dark spots, and add in bumpy areas using tiny circles. Fill in the eye, and lightly shade under the lizard's belly and neck.

Young Gila monsters can eat as much as one-half of their body weight in one feeding. If you weigh 90 pounds, that would mean eating 45 pounds of food for one meal!

The Komodo Dragon is native to islands north of Australia. It is the largest land reptile and the

① Start with a blunt oblong shape for the body.

This monitor lizard can be up to 10 feet (3.1 meters) long, including the tail, and weigh 365 pounds (164 kilograms).

② For the tail, draw a gently sloping line starting at the highest point of the body. Add a thick shape for the neck and ovals for the upper right legs.

The Komodo dragon digs a burrow for laying eggs, and a clutch of eggs can number from a single egg to thirty. Hatchlings can be 8 inches (20 centimeters) to 19 inches (48 centimeters) long.

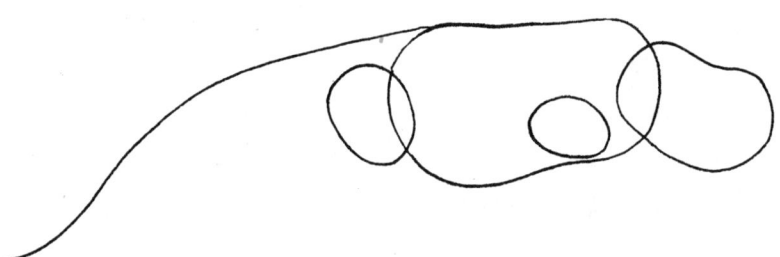

③ Add four more ovals for the lower legs, including those partially visible behind the neck and tail. Sketch a pointed egg shape for the head, and finish the outline of the tail.

The adult dragon uses its tail to knock down victims, which can be younger dragons. The young dragons climb trees hunting for smaller lizards, rats, mice, or birds to eat.

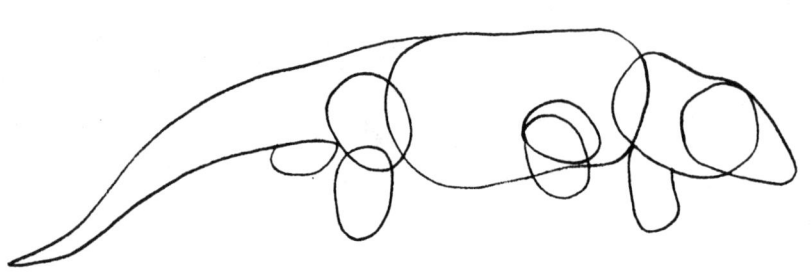

oldest living lizard species, having evolved before the dinosaurs.

---

④ Draw rounded shapes for the heavy feet and a slightly curving line down the center of the head, dividing the two sides. Add the eye.

The dragons are meat eaters and will attack deer, pigs, water buffalo, or even horses, though they regularly scavenge on dead animals.

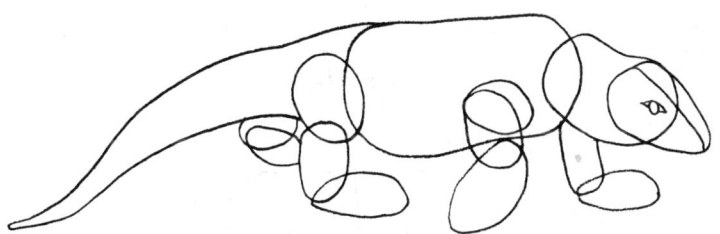

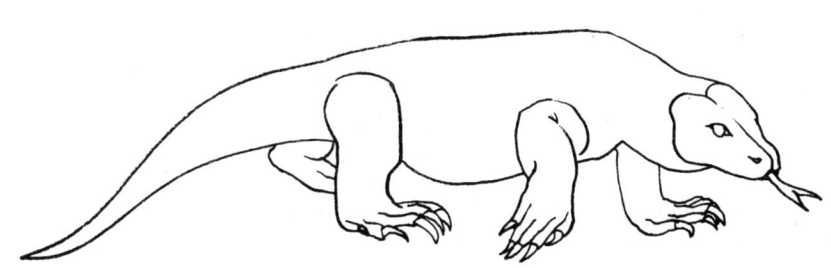

⑤ Smooth the joints between sections of the legs, head, and body, and draw in toes and claws within the guideline shapes. Refine the head shape, add a nostril and forked tongue, and erase unnecessary lines.

Like snakes, the dragons "smell" with their tongues, which are bright yellow. The claws are helpful for digging up the mounds where large birds lay their eggs. The younger animals use their claws to climb trees as well. (Adult dragons are too heavy to climb trees.)

⑥ Shade along the edges of the muscle in the tail, and draw in wrinkles in the thick skin. Shade under the body, far legs, and head. Darken the eye and claws.

The skin of the adult dragon is beaded with small bony bumps, and its color is dusty brown or gray. Young dragons are brightly colored, with forelegs and tails banded in brown and yellow, a yellow-green head and neck, and even brick-red rings along dark brown sides.

MORE SCIENCE: The shape of the Komodo dragon's teeth is more like sharks' teeth than like those of other reptiles. Even if its prey escapes after being bitten, the septic saliva of the dragon will cause severe infection and, shortly after, death.

The Boa Constrictor whose name means to tighten or squeeze, kills its prey by tightening on its chest to suffocate it, or by crushing

① Draw two vertical lines for the tree that the boa is clinging to. Then, one on top of the other, draw an irregular rounded shape, a sideways teardrop (the head), and a flattened oval.

The boa constrictor lives in tropical forests from Mexico south to Argentina. It spends a good portion of its time in trees, which it climbs by hugging the trunk with its tail, then reaching up to hook its head around a higher branch. The boa constrictor then releases its tail and pulls up the rest of its body.

② Add a smaller oval above the top one, centered on the tree guidelines. With curving lines, connect the two lower shapes, then the head shape to the lowest oval. Continue the line from the head inside the largest oval to form a loop, making a donut shape.

The boa constrictor hunts at dusk for small animals, including rats, birds, bats, lizards, and sometimes small caimans (crocodile relatives). When people keep boa constrictors as pets, the snakes will usually eat mice, rats, guinea pigs, rabbits, or chicks.

③ Between the top two ovals, draw the thin tail tip curving around the tree. Draw the eye and suggest the upper and lower jaws. Between the jaws, draw a jelly-bean shape for the rat's body.

Like all snakes, the boa constrictor swallows its prey whole. It can swallow animals thicker than the width of its mouth because its lower jaws are two separate bones. As the prey is pulled in, the ligament between the right and left sides of the jaws stretches and the prey can be swallowed.

with its coils. Full-grown at about the length of the average sedan, a boa constrictor is about one-third the size of its largest snake relatives.

---

④ Add the tail and hind feet of the rat, as well as the snake's nostril. Draw a thin line from the topmost coil through the coil above the snake's head for the backbone ridge.

While its sight may not be as keen as that of some other animals, the boa can feel the heat from the body of a bird or mammal through openings along its lips. Through these pits, the most sensitive heat receptors we know in animals, the boa can tell the direction of possible prey as well as how far away it is.

⑤ Erase unneeded lines, and refine the head shape. Draw in the diamond-shaped pattern on the body, making sure the shapes follow the roundness of the coils. Draw curved streaks on the lower coil. Refine the rat's feet, then add the claws.

This snake is a help to farmers in Brazil by keeping rats under control. Farmers are usually glad to see it coiled under the eaves of a barn.

⑥ Finish this drawing by darkly shading the tree. Make the pattern of the snake's scales with sets of curving lines that cross each other to make tiny diamonds. Darken the snake's eye, leaving a highlight, and darken the larger diamond pattern, leaving a white area in the center. Don't forget to add fur texture and shading to the rat.

These snakes mate in early spring, and up to 60 young are born between May and August. The mother leaves immediately, and the babies, which are already over 12 inches (30 centimeters) long, must start to find their own food right away.

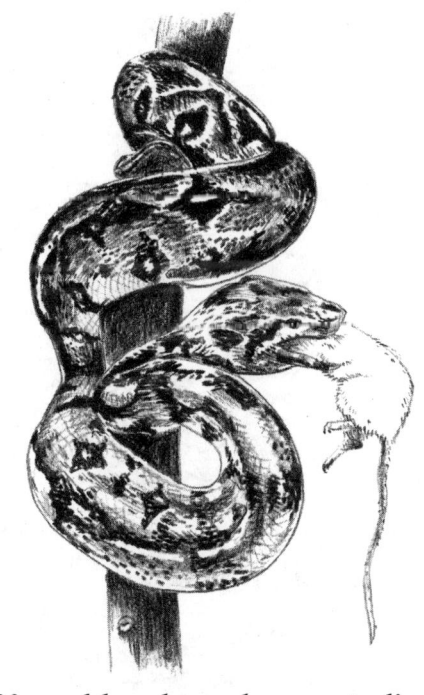

MORE SCIENCE: The boa constrictor continues to grow all its life and has been known to live for 30 years in captivity.

The Australian Frilled Lizard like other lizards, lives in all the warmer parts of the world.

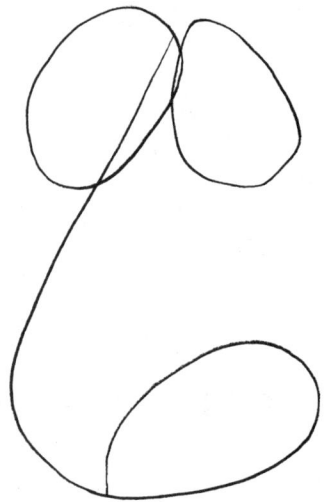

① Start with two egg shapes, overlapping slightly. Near the top of the left shape, draw a straight line down what will be the lizard's back, then curve it into a large oval loop.

Most lizards are good climbers, and their tails support them when draped over a branch and help them balance as they run. The tail can also be a storage place for extra fat to keep the lizard alive while it hibernates.

② At the top of the straight line, construct a small box for the head. Hang a long oval from the backbone to form the body, with two smaller ovals that will be the upper legs.

Unlike its snake relatives, most lizards have movable eyelids, legs, and external ears, which help them find the insects that form the largest part of their diet.

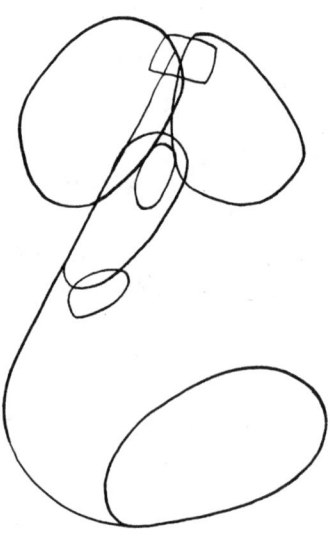

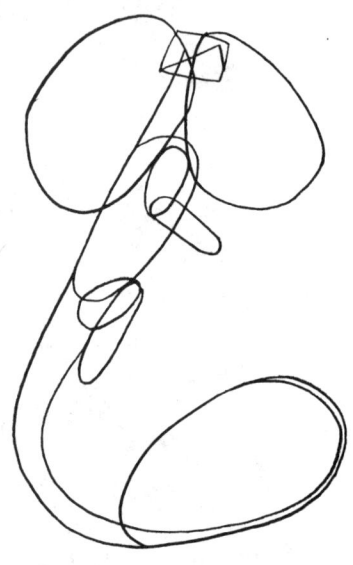

③ Draw an angled line within the box for the lizard's snout. Add long ovals for the lower legs, and complete the underside of the long, tapering tail.

A lizard has many ways of defending itself. It will first change color and stay very still. Then, if it is unable to run, this lizard puffs up its body to look larger, opens its mouth to hiss, and raises a special collar of skin, which is usually folded flat along its neck.

Similar to other reptiles, this lizard's skin has no sweat or oil glands, which gives it a dry, often dusty surface. A special characteristic of this and many other lizard species is the ability to drop their tails and regrow them.

④ Draw the eye and nostril, and within the triangle shape in the head, draw another triangle for the open mouth. Sketch rounded shapes that are the guidelines for the lizard's long toes.

This is one of a group of lizards called the "chisel teeth." While most lizards have teeth that are a part of the jawbone, the frilled lizard's teeth are attached to the surface of special bones. The teeth in front grow together and are flat, making them similar to the incisors of a rabbit or a rat.

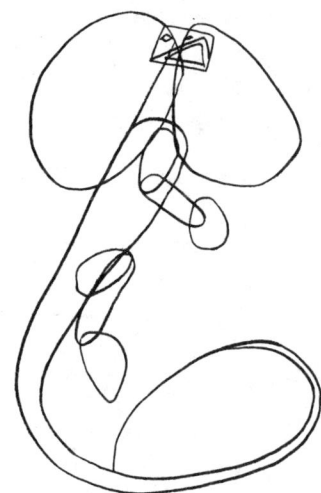

⑤ Refine the head shape, and sketch in the throat area and the bump for the crest over the farther eye. Render the frill more like a floppy leaf: make fold lines come out from behind the head, and draw in jagged frill edges. Sketch the toes, and smooth the leg joints. Erase unnecessary lines.

The lizard "smells" with its tongue, like a snake. When exploring its surroundings, it touches its tongue to the ground or other surface. Then, when the tongue touches a special place on the roof of the lizard's mouth, the information of smell or taste goes to the brain.

⑥ Give this lizard a branch to cling to with short and long straight lines. Darken its eye, mouth, and claws. Give the body a speckled surface with short dark and light strokes that make the rough scales. Add scales to the legs, head, and feet, as well as the frill. On the frill, leave the upper sides of the folds white, then darken the lower shadowed folds. The scales on the tail get smaller toward the tip until the end is solidly filled in.

Unlike snakes, lizards also use their tongues to lap water and their teeth to grasp and chew prey.

21

The Jackson's Chameleon is part of a family of tree-dwelling lizards that live in Africa, India, and

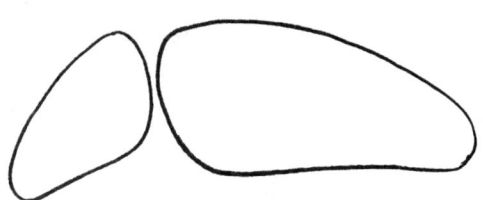

① Start with two rounded triangles, the smaller about half the size of the larger.

This lizard is particularly adapted to blend with its leafy green surroundings. Its body is tall but flat, and it moves very slowly. Some chameleons of this type may sway gently on a branch if disturbed, as a leaf would.

② Add a long line extending smoothly from the right end of the body triangle and ending in a spiral. Add two ovals for the upper legs. Make a large loop at the left as a guideline for the horns and a teardrop shape for the eye structure, called a turret.

The chameleon's tail can wrap around a tree branch for support while it searches for spiders, insects, or scorpions. The larger specimens may even feed on small birds or mice.

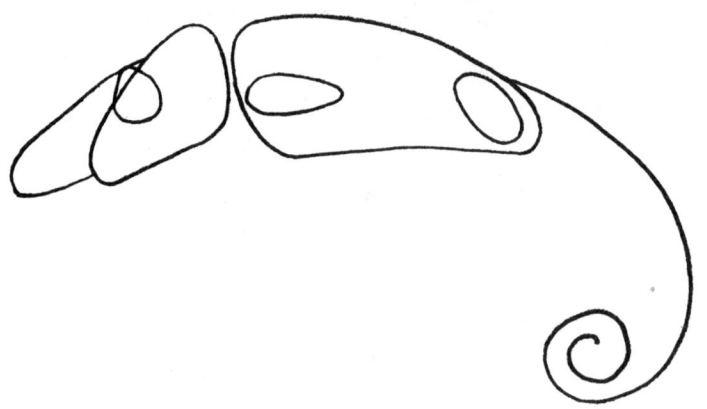

③ Above the turret, draw a circular shape that is the edge of a shieldlike collar. Add the mouth and long ovals for the lower legs. Finally, extend the bottom line of the body shape to form the lower edge of the spiral tail.

Though it moves slowly, this chameleon can shoot out a tongue—longer than its head and body!—with sticky mucus on the end that traps its prey and brings it to the mouth. It chews with teeth attached to the edge of its upper jaw.

Madagascar. They are about 5 to 6 inches (13 to 15 centimeters) long and are known for their ability to change color rapidly.

---

④ Attach the head to the body, and draw the curving crest that extends along the back from the neck to the tail. Draw in the tapered horns with their bases covered by skin. Add rounded guidelines for the feet.

The three horns are used when a male chameleon is protecting his territory. The males are known to have long fights.

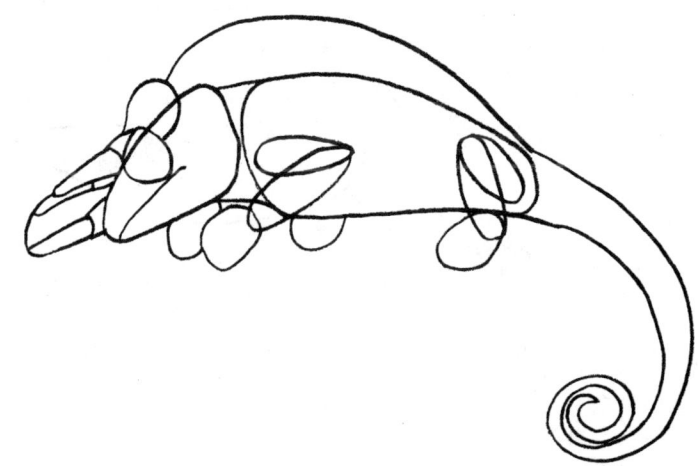

⑤ Draw in the toes on the feet and shape the legs. Add the small oval for the eye at the tip of its turret. Erase unnecessary lines. You should have a complete outline of your chameleon.

The eyes are on turrets that move independently of each other, so that the left eye can be looking forward while the right eye searches behind, above, or below. This is probably why the animal can strike its prey so accurately when hunting.

⑥ Shade the side of the crest, and give it a toothed edge similar to a leaf. Continue the uneven edge along the top of the tail. Along the jaws, draw in tiny flat and round scales. Darken the eye, and shade its turret and the horns so they look cone shaped. Shade the undersides of the body, head, and tail, and give the chameleon an overall speckled effect. Draw in a curving branch for the chameleon to rest on.

This chameleon can be a rich green with dark flecks, but if displaying for a female or hiding itself from a predator, it can change to nearly black or nearly white, or colors in between, in only a few minutes.

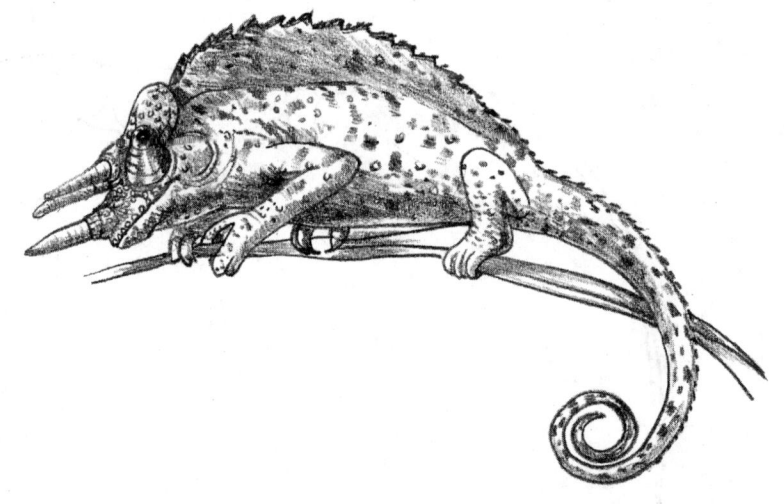

The American Chameleon of the south and southeast United States is considered

① Draw the body as a bullet with a slight curve up at each end. The teardrop head should be in line with the body curve, but not touching it.

These animals are about 6 inches (16 centimeters) long, including the tail. They make interesting pets as long as they can be kept warm and provided with moisture and live insects.

② Bring a line from the head along the back, then curving downward to form the top of the slender tail. Draw the upper leg shapes.

The long, round tail is important for balance and as an aid in climbing. Like most lizards, the chameleon can release its tail when caught. The tail end jerks and bounces to get the attention of a predator, while the lizard escapes and eventually grows a new tail.

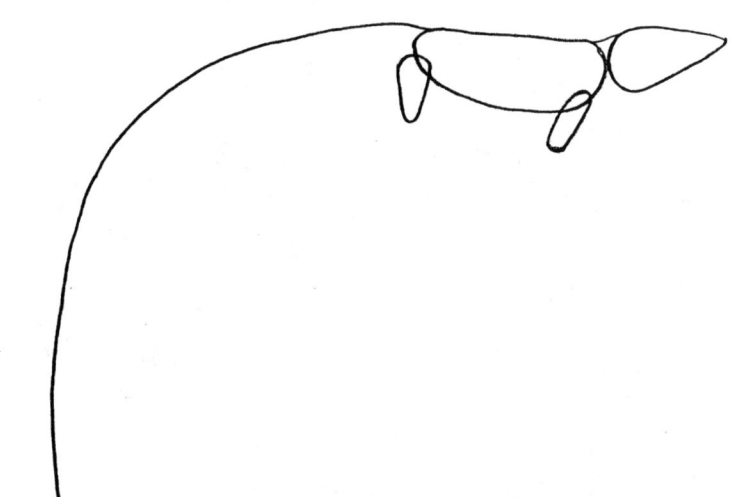

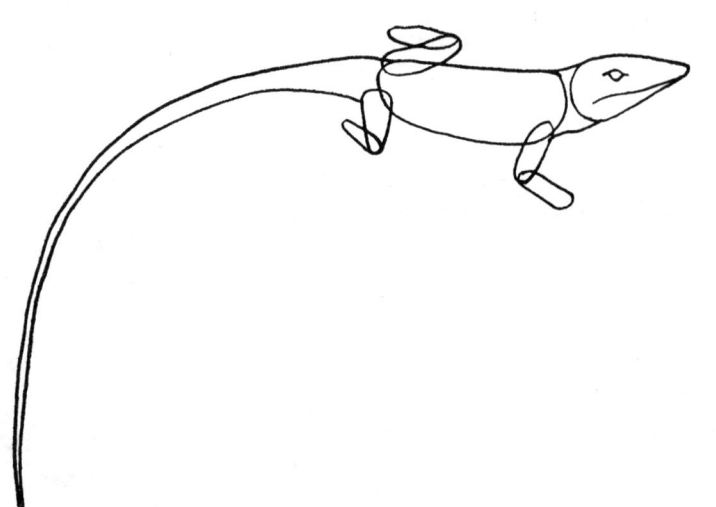

③ Add the far upper leg and all the bent lower legs. Sketch the lower edge of the neck and tail, and add the eye and mouth.

Unlike other lizards, the American chameleon male can extend its throat into a flat fan shape that becomes bright red, orange, or yellow. It is thought this display is for attracting a female or scaring off a rival.

a farmer's helper because it eats flies, mosquitoes, and caterpillars, stalking them like a cat hunts mice.

---

④ Make broad shapes, overlapping the lower legs, for the feet. Draw in the nostril, and begin to shape the body near the visible foreleg.

This lizard is an excellent climber and, using its wide, flat toes, can even grasp vertical or overhanging surfaces. Its toe pads have crosswise ridges that help it grasp.

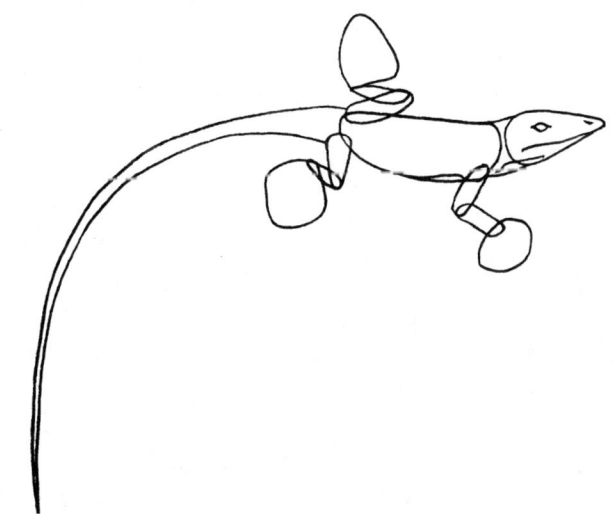

⑤ Using the guidelines, draw in the toes with wide tips and claws. Erase unneeded lines.

In the wild, this lizard becomes very active in the late morning when it races around in the foliage, hunting or fighting. It leaps 2 or 3 feet (61 to 91 centimeters) from one branch to another, and can launch itself out of a tree down several stories to the ground.

⑥ This lizard is called a chameleon because it has the ability to change color quickly and completely. It is generally darker on top and lighter underneath. Use the side of your pencil to give the animal a smooth-looking surface. Add a rough edge and tiny dark spots to the tail. Fill in the eye and claws, and place more spots on its back.

Unlike other animals that change color to blend in with backgrounds, the chameleon seems to change color because of its activity, excitement level, or the temperature of the environment. When it is fighting or courting a mate, it is usually green. In colder temperatures, it takes on the darker colors. At any time, though, the animal can blend its colors into an amazing range of combinations.

The Giant Land Tortoise is found on the Galápagos Islands west of Ecuador in

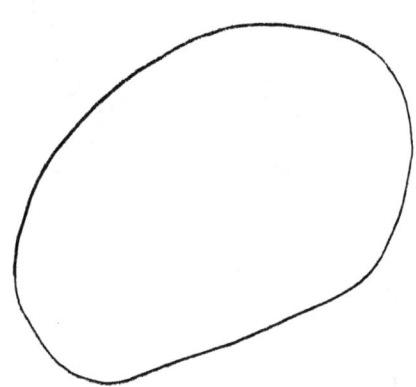

① Start with an oval, tilted up at the right end and slightly flattened on the underside.

These giant tortoises are the last of several similar species that scientist Charles Darwin studied more than 100 years ago. Because they were on nearby but separate islands and showed differences in size and shape, Darwin was encouraged in his theories about ways animals adapt and change according to their surroundings.

② Draw the boxlike shape for the head, overlapping the body shape. Upper leg shapes should be thick and angle outward from beneath the body.

These tortoises sometimes use abandoned burrows of some mammals as protection from the dry heat of the day or the cold in winter. However, they are excellent diggers and have been found in burrows as long as a school bus.

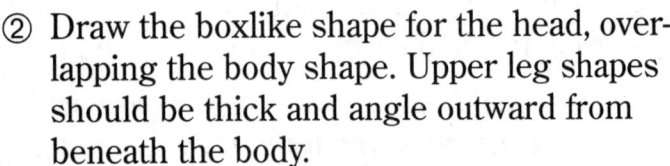

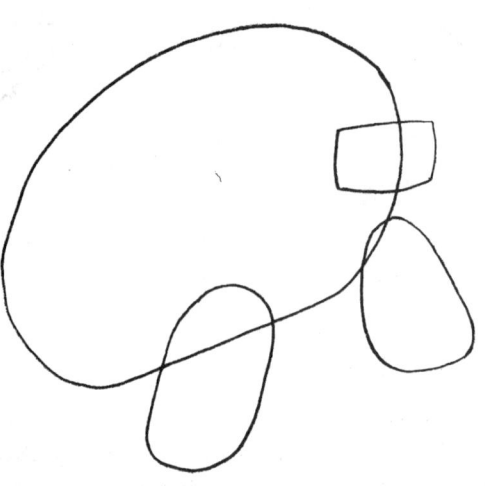

③ Add rounded shapes for the hind feet. Draw the thick, wedge-shaped front feet turned slightly inward.

In spite of the weight they must carry, tortoises are good climbers. Hooking their forelegs over rocks to hold to a slope, they push forward with their hind legs. Their dens or burrows are usually dug in soft overhanging banks above a stream and require a steep climb to enter.

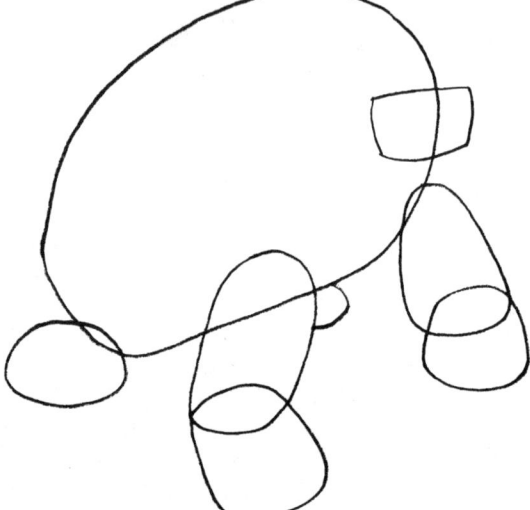

South America and is one of the largest living land tortoises. It can grow to a length of 4 feet (1.2 meters) and weigh as much as 500 pounds (225 kilograms).

④ Draw a wavy line—like a ruffle—from the hind foot up to behind the head to mark the bottom edge of the shell. Draw flaring lines that form the upper and lower edges of the neck, and add the eye, nostril, and beak. Mark off a slightly triangular space between the front legs for the shell.

This kind of turtle has an extension of the lower shell that comes up below the neck. While the undershell "bumper" probably protects the extended head and neck from below, the tortoise sometimes uses it to bump the female during courting or to ram a rival male and overturn him.

⑤ Add a ruffled line above the first wavy line to show the shell's thickness. Then draw in the sections of the bumpy scutes, or scales, of the back. Continue to detail the lower shell. Draw in the thick, wide claws. Smooth the sections of the legs and feet, and refine the shape of the shell and head. Erase unnecessary lines.

Like all turtles with heavy shells, this one moves very slowly. It has been clocked at about 4 miles (6.4 kilometers) a day.

⑥ Use dark hatching to show that the edge of the shell projects above the neck and head area. Notice how the short, thick lines follow the curve of the body below the shell. Fill in the shell sections as shown. The skin is wrinkled and dry, so draw wobbly lines for the neck and around the tops of the legs. On the legs, tough scales should stand out like irregular paving stones, except around the claws. Darken between and shade one side of each claw, and darken the small eye and nostril.

While the giant land tortoise grows throughout its life, it grows more slowly as it gets older.

The Warty Newt is an amphibian, which means it needs a moist environment and spends part of its life in the

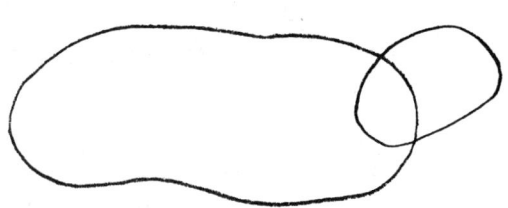

① Start with a slightly bent oval for the body with a smaller overlapping oval for the head.

Newts are like reptiles in that their skins do not stretch as they grow. Instead, they shed them regularly.

② Add a rectangular guideline box slightly overlapping the body shape. Draw small ovals for the upper hind legs and front leg.

These newts change their appearance dramatically in the spring at mating time, when the male swims and displays his bright-colored fins for the female. At other times of the year, the fins are much smaller, and the colors on the body and fins are more subdued.

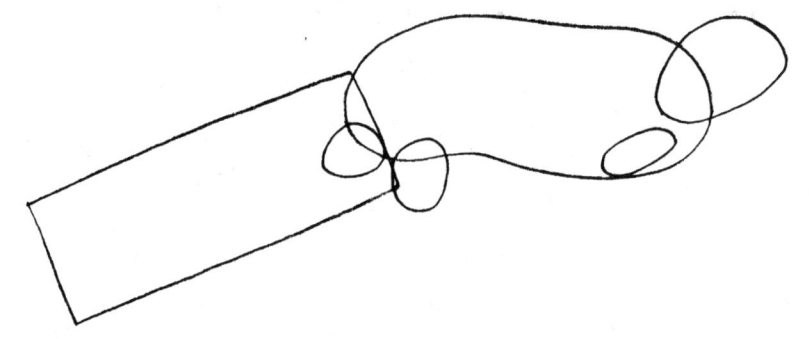

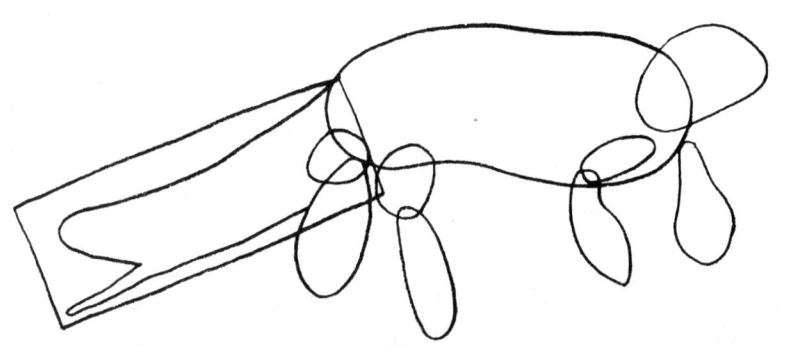

③ Add paddle shapes for the lower legs and feet, and draw the ribbonlike tail within the guideline box.

These animals may seem a good meal to forest animals. However, if they are disturbed, they exude a sticky poison from glands on their head, back, and tail. If this newt is eaten, it can kill a small animal.

water. The largest of all the European newts, the warty newt can be as long as 6½ inches (17 centimeters) for the females and 5¾ inches (15 centimeters) for the male.

---

④ Bring a wavy line from the head along the back, and continue it as an uneven line above the tail. Draw in the toes—five on the rear feet and four on the front feet.

This newt is swimming and displaying for the female. His back and tail fins have grown and are now edged with red, contrasting with the black-spotted brown skin of the body. He bounds along the stream bottom in front of the female, twisting, turning, and fluttering his fins to attract her.

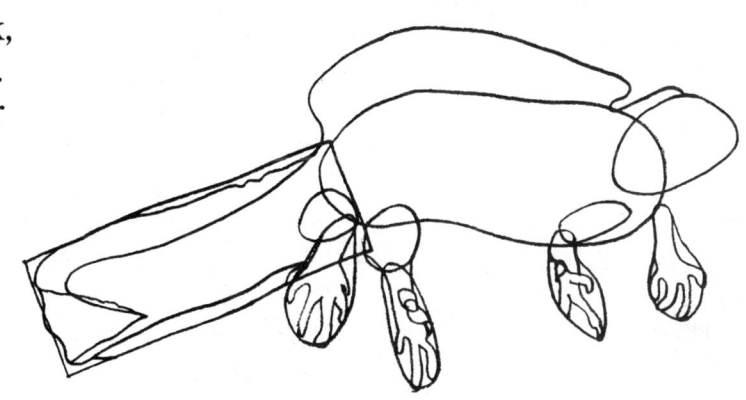

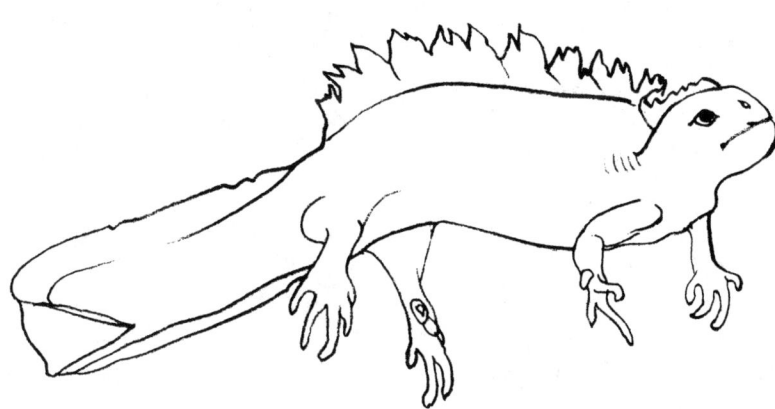

⑤ Draw in the eye, nostril, and mouth. Add the irregular edge of the head and back fins. Smooth the connections of leg joints and legs to the body. Erase all unneeded lines.

When the male has the female's attention, he may nudge her sides with his nose, or even press his nose against hers. He then deposits clusters of spermatophores on the pond floor. If she accepts his offer, the female covers the sperm clusters with her body and takes them into her body, where they fertilize her eggs.

⑥ Finish by shading its underside and the fins where they attach to the body. Shade the area around the eye and the legs, leaving the edges lighter. Show the bumps on the skin with irregular ovals. Add light hatching across the tail and body as shown.

The female lays her eggs and attaches them to stones or stems of water plants. They hatch in about two weeks as larvae with gills. By the end of the summer, their internal lungs have formed, and the young newts climb out of the pond and find hiding places under logs or stones.

The Gulf Coast Toad

like other toads, begins life with gills like a fish but changes into a lunged animal as an adult. Toads have characteristics of

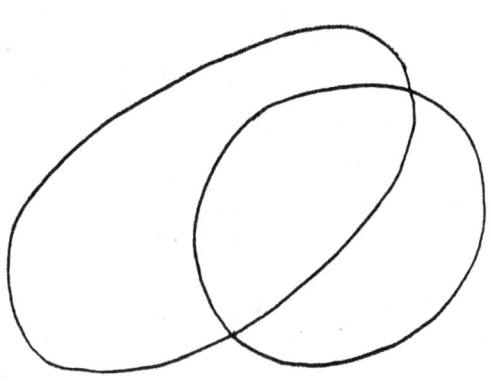

① Start with a circle overlapped by a tilted oval for the vocal pouch and the body.

Two hundred different species of toads are found all over the world where there is enough water, except in Australia and Antarctica. The Gulf Coast toad lives in the American south and grows from 3½ to 5 inches (9 to 13 centimeters) long.

② Draw in two small circles for the eye bumps and flower-petal shapes for the upper foreleg and visible hind leg.

Toads hunt for insects that are most active at night—beetles, moths, cutworms, crickets, snails, and slugs. The orange or golden eyes are large and can dilate until they are nearly black, perfect for evening hunting.

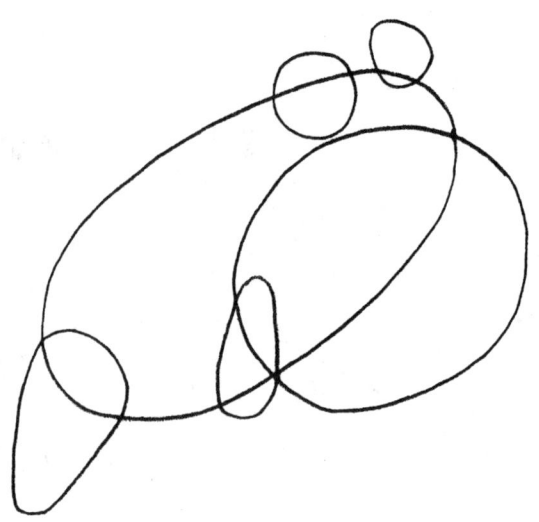

③ Continue with ovals for the lower legs in front and a rough circle for the rear leg. Add a seed shape for the eye opening and a line for the edge of the farther eye.

Most toads, as well as frogs, hatch from eggs as tadpoles with gills and tails, looking like fat-bodied dark fish. In a few weeks the arms and legs, hidden at first, grow out, the tail is absorbed into the body, and eyelids develop as the eyes move up toward the top of the head. The tadpole's mouth, a hard scraper for collecting small water plants off the stream rocks, becomes soft and broad. The process from tadpole to Gulf Coast toad takes about six weeks.

both fishes and reptiles, but only toads and frogs have long, powerful hind legs for leaping and swimming.

④ Add the lower eyelid, top of the head, nostrils, and mouth. Sketch guidelines for the feet, making sure they are large enough.

The toad has a special tongue attached at the front of its mouth. When it sees movement of something that may be food, it shoots the tongue out as far as 2 inches (5 centimeters). The tongue's sticky end catches an insect and tosses it back into the open mouth almost too quickly for a person to see.

⑤ Inside the feet guidelines, form the toes—the five hind toes are webbed. Behind the eye, add the eardrum. Erase unneeded lines, then add the skin folds.

Both male and female toads have a voice, though the male's is almost always louder. Air comes into the mouth through the nostrils, and some is captured in vocal sacs that puff up the throat. These sacs help to make the sound loud as air is pushed past the vocal cords. Each species has its own sound, so males and females can find each other at mating time.

⑥ Finish the toad by lightly shading and making speckles and bumps on its skin. Darken the nostril and toe tips. The eye should be very dark with a small white highlight.

Though the toad may look like a nice bite for a fox or wolf, it will secrete a whitish fluid when grabbed in an animal's mouth. The liquid burns and tastes so bitter, the toad may be freed almost immediately. The toxin is not dangerous to humans unless it gets into the mouth or an eye.

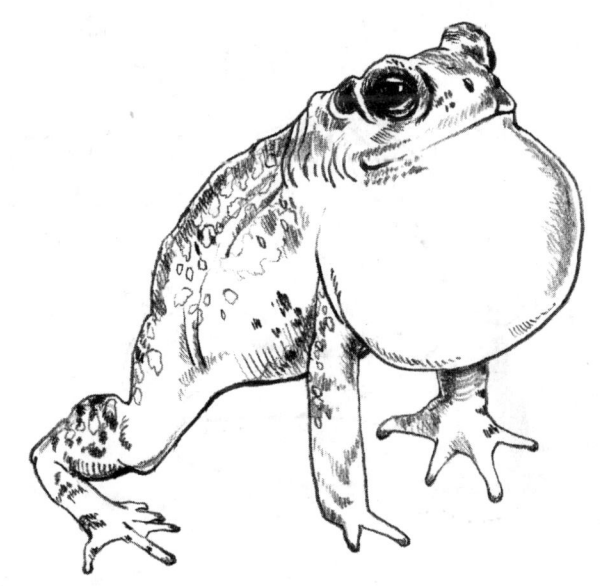

31

The South American Pygmy Marsupial Frog

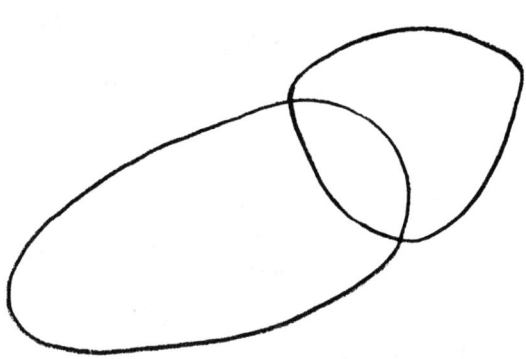

① The body should be a slender oval. Make the head a fat, rounded triangle, overlapping the oval.

Like other frogs, this one must keep its skin moist so it can absorb the liquid it needs. It lives in and around air plants that perch high in the forest canopy on top of other plants. These plants get the water and nutrients they need from the air, thus, their name. The water is collected at the bases of their broad leaves.

② Add circles for the eyes and long, slender ovals for the first joint of each hind and foreleg.

The adult pygmy marsupial frog uses its long legs, not to swim, but to hunt its prey: moths, flying cockroaches, flies, and other insects. These frogs can jump more than 17 times their own length!

③ Draw in the nostril and curved upper eyelids. Sketch more ovals for the lower legs.

Like many frogs, this one has brilliant jewellike eyes, in this case, a gold color. This female frog is slender now, but she will be quite bulky when the eggs she lays are tucked into a pouch on her back. In this pouch, the eggs will go through the tadpole stage, protected from drying out and drastic temperature changes by the female's ability to move them to safety.

one of 640 species, is a 2-inch-long (5 centimeters) tree frog that can live its whole life and never touch the ground.

---

④ Sketch curved shapes for the hind feet, and form the line for the bend in the left rear leg. Draw broad paddles for guidelines for the front feet.

Like most tree frogs, this one has broad, flat toe tips that help it cling to the smooth, wet surfaces of leaves. The bottoms of these pads are a spongy fiber, allowing the frog to cling to leaves upside down!

⑤ Draw in the toes and the pupils of the eyes. With curving lines, show the bulging shapes of the eyes under the lids. Smooth the joints of the legs, then erase the unneeded lines.

When the young have grown to about ½ inch (1.2 centimeters) long and their legs are fairly well developed, the female leaves them so they can start hunting insects on their own.

⑥ The skin of this frog is rather bumpy and sprinkled with dark markings that disguise it among leaves. Shade the legs and feet where they overlap, and shade the eye bulges and lower edge of the snout. Darken the pupil of the eye, and give the colored part some tone, leaving a white highlight in the eye for the shine.

This specimen is light brown, speckled with darker brown. Like other frogs, it can change color to pale green, matching its leafy home.

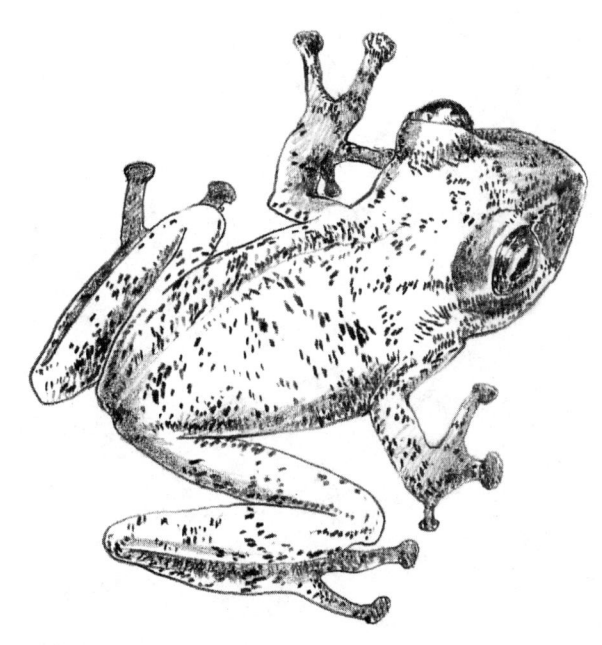

The Chinese Spiny Newt is one of a group of small amphibians that live in damp

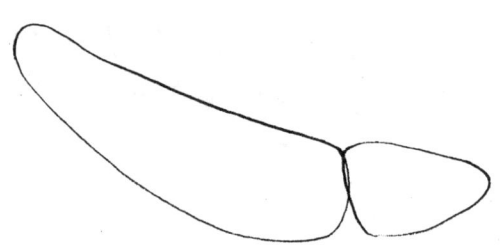

① Draw the body as a curved club shape and the head as a fat, rounded triangle.

This animal is about 6 inches (15 centimeters) long and lives on insects, slugs, snails, and worms. It needs a damp environment such as a woodland floor and gets its oxygen through its skin.

② Bring a line from near the triangle's tip, curving with the body, then bending upward into a long *S* for the upraised tail. Add ovals for the upper legs, a bump on the head for the farther eye, and a half-oval for the nearer eye.

This newt is in a defensive pose, probably threatened by a snake, bird, or small mammal. It is lashing its tail as a warning.

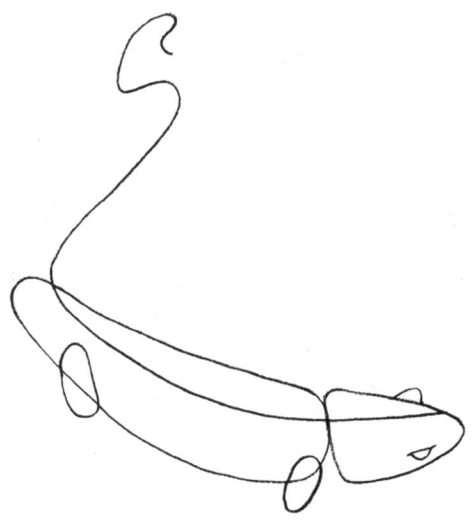

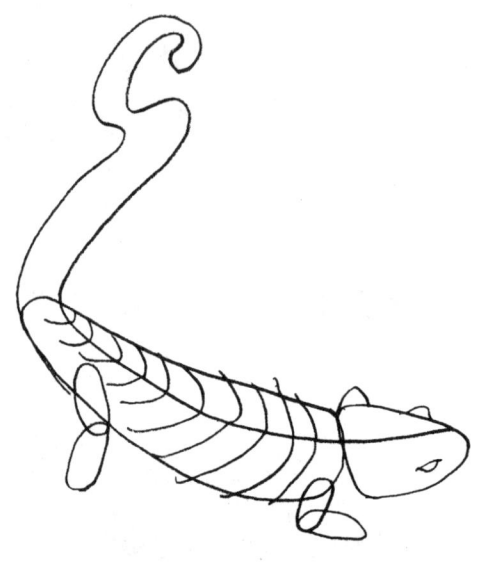

③ From the lower edge of the body, draw a second *S*-shaped line to form a wide ribbon-shaped tail with a rounded end. Along the backbone line, draw the ribs, pointing toward the head and getting smaller toward the tail. Add lower leg shapes, including the corner of the far front foot.

The prominent ribs have poison glands at their tips. If an attacker swallows or grasps this newt, the ribs poke through the glands and skin, carrying the poison into the predator's mouth.

environments, have a smooth (nonscaly) skin, and are active at night. New species of newts are still being discovered today, especially in the South American tropics.

④ Add fan shapes for the feet, and refine the rear edge of the head. Detail the lower edge of the body behind the visible hind foot.

Unlike other amphibians (frogs and toads) who look totally different from their early stages of growth to adulthood, the newborn newt looks very similar to the adult. As it develops, the newt loses featherlike gills around the head, as well as texture in the skin and tail fin.

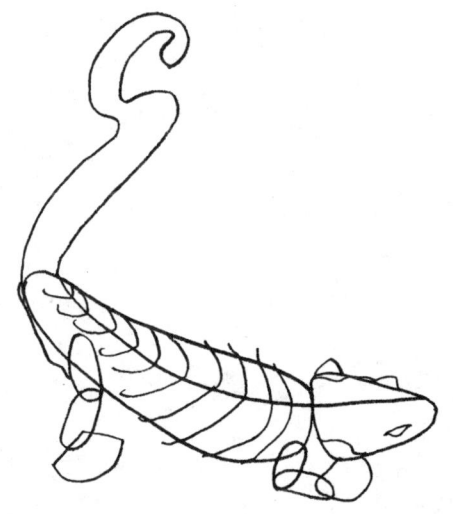

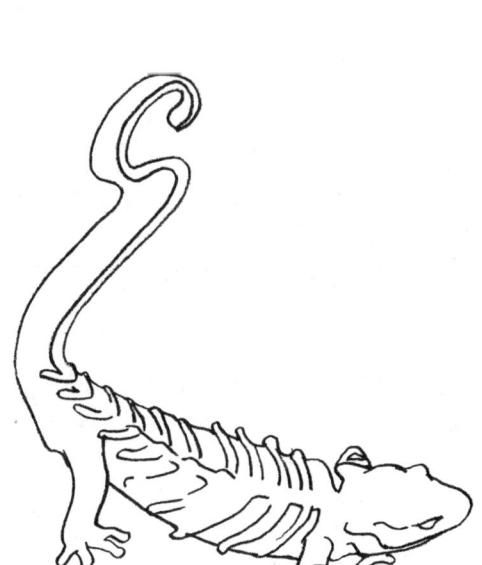

⑤ Draw in a ridge line behind the eye, and form the toes. Finish the outline of the ribs, and add a broken, bumpy line for the backbone. Add a line that follows the edge of the tail, and smooth the joints of the legs. Erase unnecessary lines.

Newts commonly raise and lash their tail when threatened. One reason is that there are poison glands in the upper edge of the tail as well as at the ribs.

⑥ Shade the tail so it has a thicker ridge on the top and seems to bend. Darken around the ribs and backbone area so they appear as ridges. Shade the underside of the head, darken the eye, and use half-circles to show the skin's bumpy texture.

This newt is dark colored, as if it has been burned. Its toe tips and rib ends are orange, and the rest of the pebbly skin is brownish black. Often bright colors like orange and yellow are a warning to birds and mammals, who know the colors belong to animals with poisonous skins.

The Texas Horned Lizard also called the horned toad, lives from Kansas south and

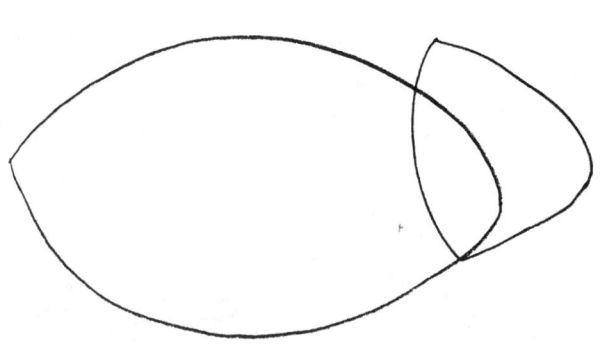

① Start with a large football shape and overlap it with a fan shape for the head.

Living in desertlike surroundings, this flat lizard uses its head like a plow and nose like a shovel to hide itself under the soil at night. During the day, it searches for ants and other insects to eat, whipping its tongue out like a toad to capture its prey.

② Add a line going beyond the length of the football, curving down slightly to the left. Draw oval shapes for the upper legs.

The horned lizard has been known to charge another lizard or snake that threatens it. If that fails, it puffs up its body and tucks its head down to extend its horns.

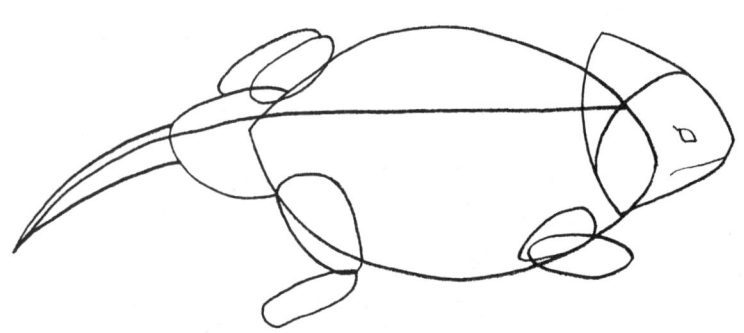

③ Draw in the lower leg shapes, the base of the tail, and the tapering tail shape. Add the line for the upper edge of the head, then add the eye and the mouth.

This lizard cannot break off its tail, but when captured, it may act as if it were dead. Predators that insist on swallowing the lizard may be severely injured when its horns or back spines pierce their throat or stomach walls.

west through Colorado and southeastern Arizona. This spiny lizard measures 4 to 4½ inches (10 to 11 centimeters) long.

④ Add ovals for the feet and a row of spikes on the back of the head, as well as two back-curving horns.

Like some other lizards, the horned lizard seems to be subject to a form of hypnosis: If stroked gently several times between the eyes, it seems to go into a deep sleep and becomes very limp.

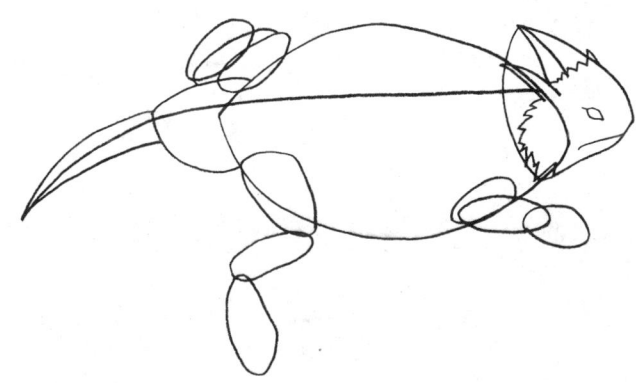

⑤ Draw in the toes and claws. Roughen the edges of the body, leg, and tail outlines with backward-facing points. Erase any extra lines, and sketch in the outlines of the dark body markings.

When shedding its skin or when annoyed, this lizard can voluntarily squirt blood from its eyes—sometimes as far as 4 feet (1.2 meters)!

⑥ Shade the horns to make them appear rounded, and add shadows of the horns on the neck. The horned lizard has a light stripe down the middle of its back and dark leaf-shaped spots, which lighten toward the center. To make the points on the skin and head stand out, darken the rear side of each one. You can use rough, short strokes to make this animal's markings stand out and emphasize its prickly surface.

This animal is light yellowish brown to brownish red or tan and gray. The darker markings may be brown or gray, and its underside is a pale cream to white with a few dark spots.

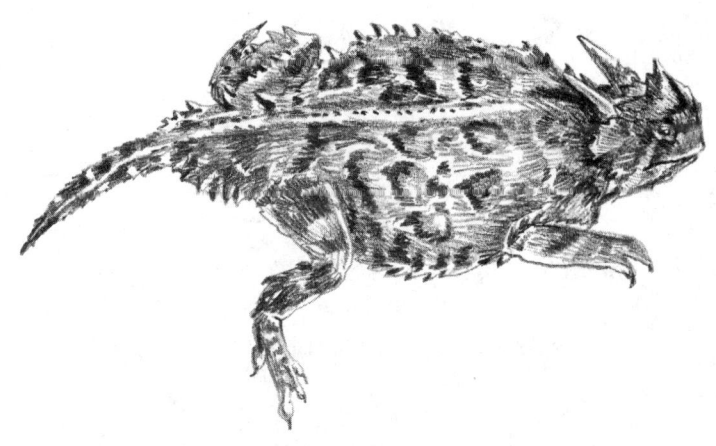

MORE SCIENCE: This species needs hot weather to hunt and eat well. When cold weather sets in, it goes into hibernation. In the spring, mating occurs, and the female lays 20 to 40 eggs in a shallow hole that she has dug.

Boulanger's Arrow Poison Frog is a small but dangerous frog

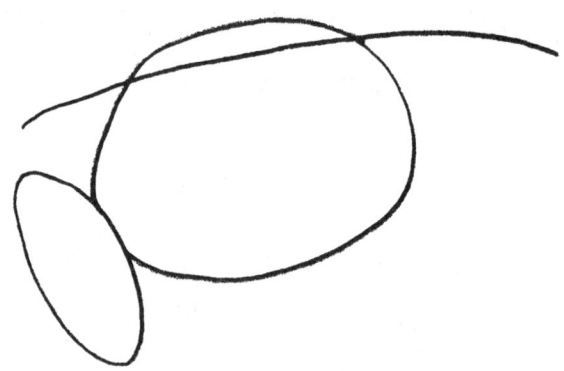

① Make the body a slightly flattened circle with a seedlike shape for the upper hind leg. Bring a gently down-curved line across the top of the circle, just above the leg shape, going beyond the circle to begin the head.

This frog advertises its poison with its bright orange and black skin. The poison varies from animal to animal. While some poisons only burn the mouth of the attacking animal, others will cause death.

② Continue the upper line, bending it backward to the body to form a slim bullet shape for the head. Show the legs on the far side of the body as partial ovals, and draw a thin oval for the upper right foreleg.

The South American natives have used the highly toxic secretions of several species of these small frogs to make hunting food easier. After stabbing the frog with a pointed stick, they heat the dead animal over a fire and collect the poison that "sweats" out.

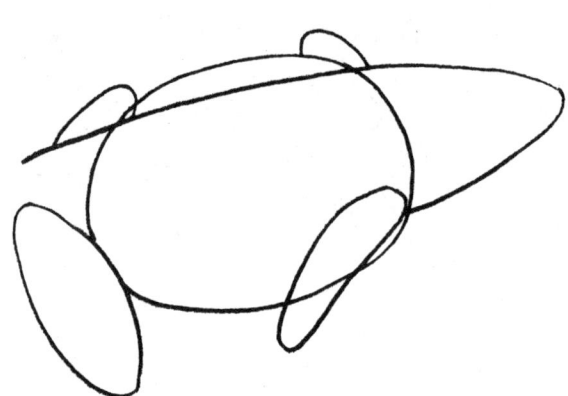

③ Add circles for the eyes and long, rounded stick shapes for the lower legs. Connect the back legs to the body.

The arrow poison frog measures only 1 to 2 inches (2.5 to 5 centimeters) long. However, its poison is so strong that one tiny frog yields enough to tip 50 arrows for hunting. When struck, prey animals are paralyzed.

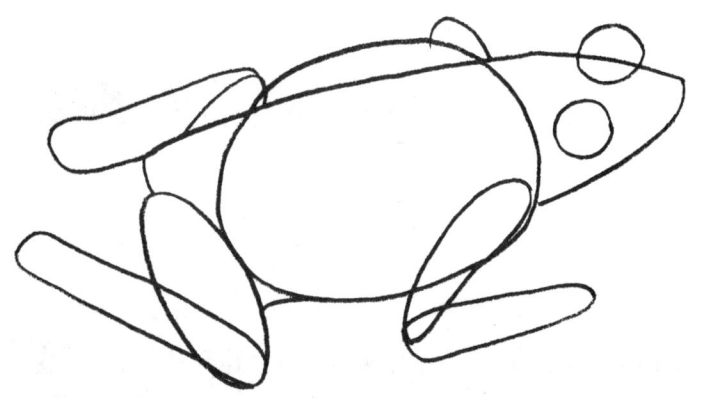

38

that lives high in the Andes mountains of Peru or Ecuador in South America.

---

④ Draw in paddle-shaped outlines for the visible front and hind feet. Don't forget the toe peeking out from the far hind foot. Then draw in the eye opening, and shape the top of the slightly lumpy back with a line going from the eye to the left hind leg.

The male arrow poison frog helps raise the young. After the eggs are laid and fertilized, they are attached to the father's back. When they hatch, the tadpoles hold on with their mouths for several weeks, depending on the father to dunk them or let rain fall on them to keep them moist.

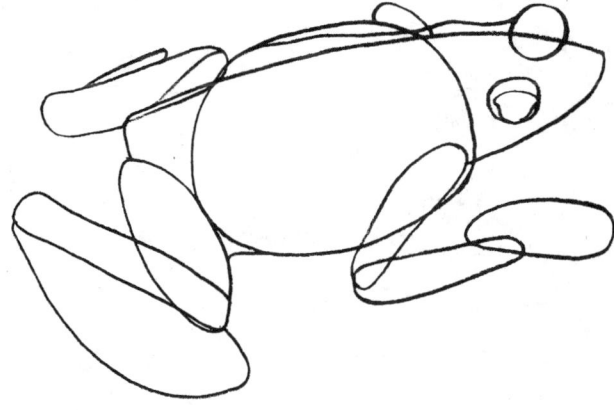

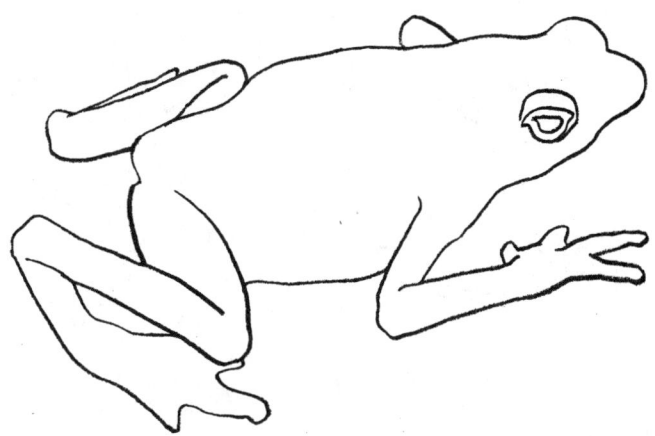

⑤ Draw in the frog's toes—the hind feet are webbed. Add the eye pupil, and smooth the joints of the legs and body. Refine the outline of the snout, jointed limbs, and belly, and erase extra guidelines.

The poison of this frog is considered the most poisonous biological toxin in the world. It can kill a person if it gets into an open wound.

⑥ Outline the lighter-colored spots on this frog, taking care to draw them so they appear to wrap around the legs, toes, and body. Fill in the background solidly, then lightly shade the lower edges of the body and limbs. Detail the ridge running along its back to the eye. If you are coloring this drawing, the lighter areas should be bright yellow-orange.

Scientists have found that, if separated from the dangerous material, an ingredient in this frog's poison is a powerful painkiller, many times more effective than the commonly used plant-based painkiller morphine.

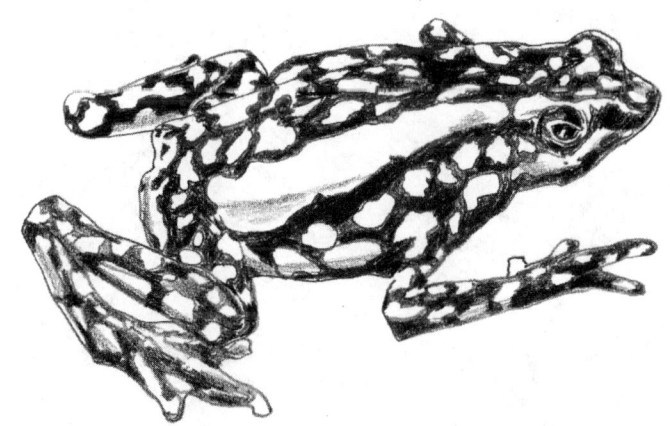

The Surinam Toad lives in the Orinoco and Amazon rivers of South America. This unusual-looking toad

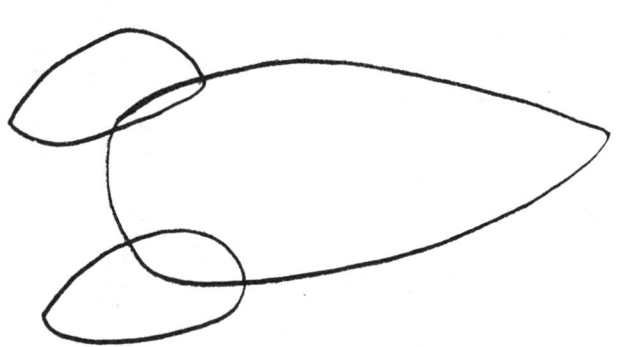

① Start with a pointed flower-petal shape, and overlap it with two smaller oval shapes.

This toad has a very flat, blackish-brown body and powerful swimming legs. It is awkward out of water, but its flexible body seems to help it move easily through the currents.

② Add fan shapes for the four feet and circles for the tiny eyes.

While most toads need large eyes that protrude from the head to watch out for predators, this one seems to see very well both above and to the side with small, lidless eyes that are nearly even with its skin.

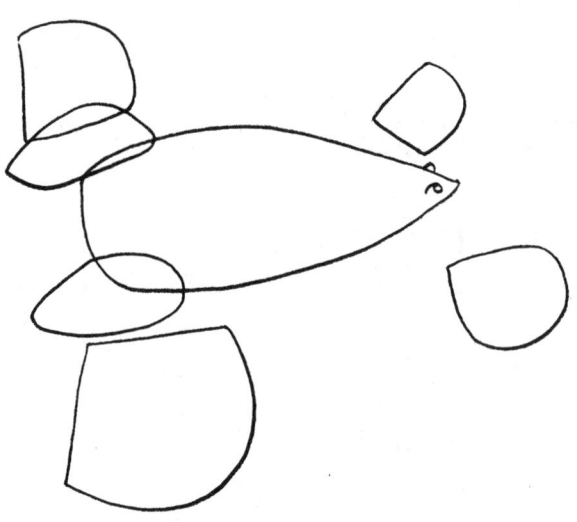

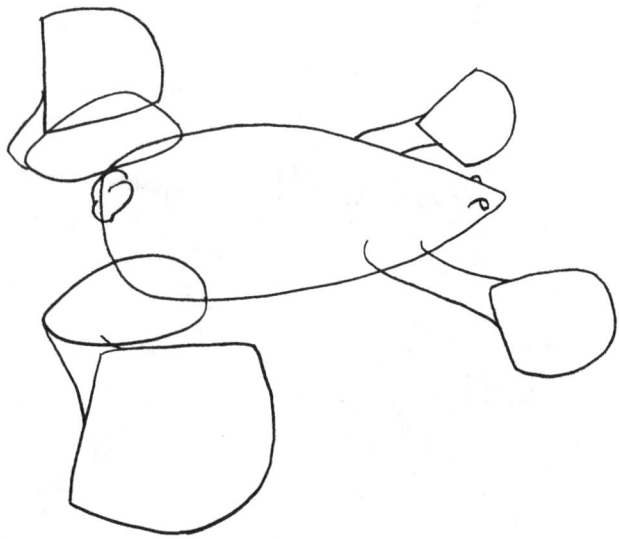

③ Connect the feet to the body using curved lines. Add the small opening between the hind legs for egg laying.

When the female lays eggs, the male fertilizes them, then helps maneuver them onto the thickened skin of her back. Hours later, the skin on the female's back swells to enclose and cover the eggs, with each one in its own pocket. The eggs stay there as the mother goes about her feeding and movements. When the tiny toads hatch, a lid opens in the mother's back and each toadlet appears and swims to the top of the pond.

has no tongue and has specially designed "fingers" to help it find food in the dark, muddy water of the river bottoms.

④ Draw in the toes, four in front and five on the hind feet. (You can't see all five toes on the far hind foot.)

The toad's long "fingers" are very flexible. They are used to sweep the mud bottom to turn up food—any animal or water insect, alive or dead.

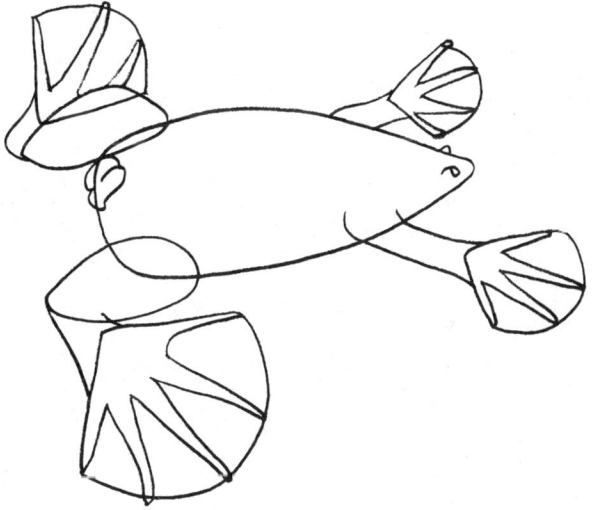

⑤ Refine the webs on the hind feet, and add short, tapered lines on the fingertips of the front feet. Erase unnecessary lines.

The star-shaped clusters at the end of the toes help the toad identify food items even in very thick mud.

⑥ Finish the drawing by darkening the eyes and shading the underside of the legs and body. The surface of the skin is covered with small bumps, and the back of this female shows a few of the egg capsules where baby toads have just hatched.

The young of the Surinam toad go through the tadpole, or polliwog, stage while still in the eggs on their mother's back.

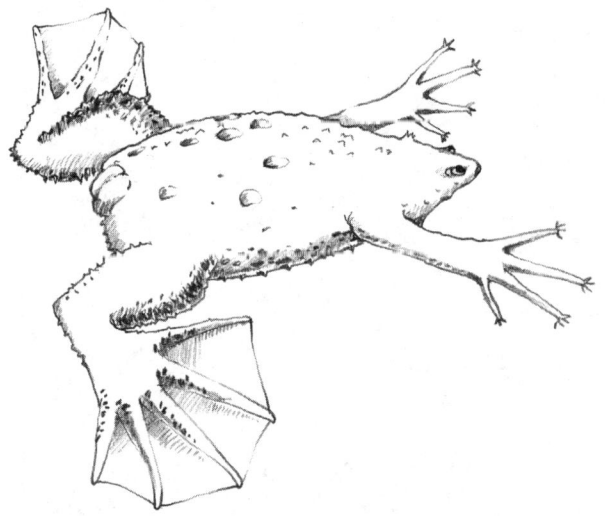

MORE SCIENCE: Females of an African relative of this tongueless toad laid fertilized eggs when exposed to the hormones of pregnant human females. This was the first reliable pregnancy test for humans, and for a while the toads were in great demand as testers.

The American Bullfrog is one of the best-known animals of the frog family. Its relatives can be found near fresh water in every

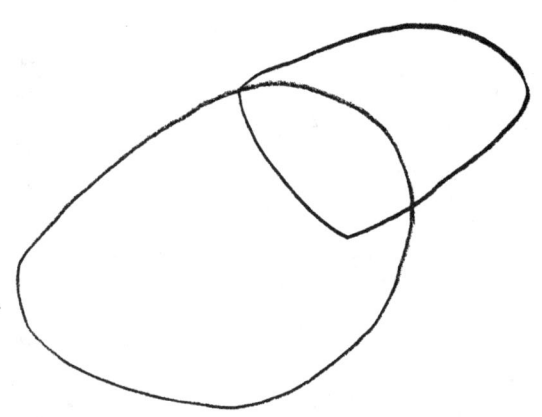

① The body is a slightly flat-sided egg. Overlap it with a smaller shape for the head.

The American bullfrog is widely used by schools and medical laboratories to study internal organs of backboned animals, and most recently, it has been used to test methods for making successful organ transplants.

② Add ovals of different sizes for the muscular hind leg, upper foreleg, and eyes. A wedge shape along the back is the outline of the upper part of the pelvis.

Frogs, partly because their eyes bulge out from their head, are considered to have the best vision among any backboned animals, except perhaps some fish. They can see in nearly all directions at once, and can distinguish colors. Their night vision is particularly good.

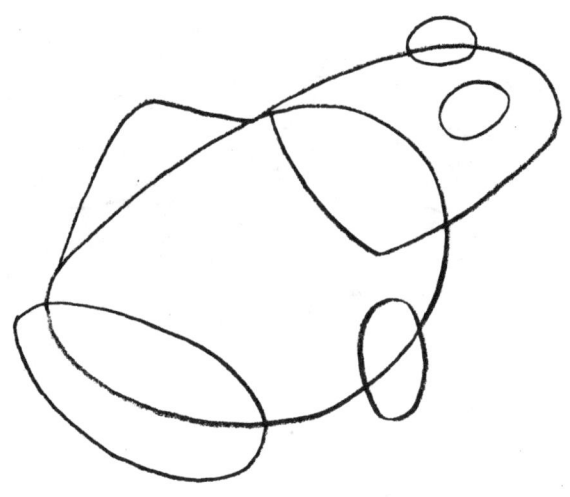

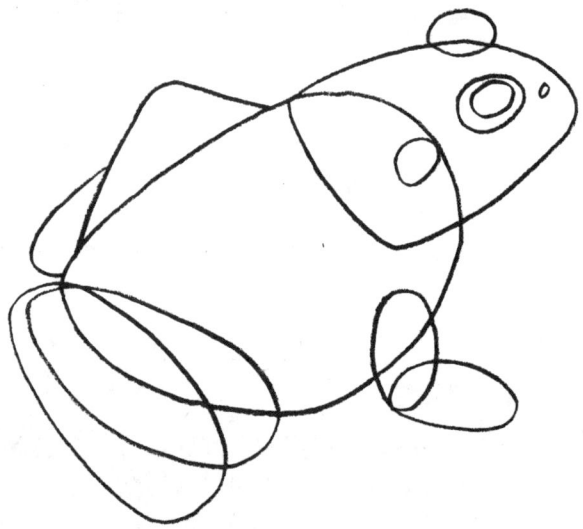

③ Continue adding ovals—a small one for the nostril, one for the opening of the eye, one for the eardrum behind the eye, and others for the lower legs. Don't forget the curved line for the left rear leg.

These animals, which grow to about 4 inches (10 centimeters) long, are food for fish when they are in the egg and as tadpoles. When grown, they are prey for birds and mammals. They eat flies, mosquitoes, snails, slugs, caterpillars, and beetles, and have been brought to farmers' fields to help control insect pests.

part of the world except in permanently frozen areas, New Zealand, Madagascar, and most of Australia.

④ To the right hind-foot ovals, add the toe tips, with webbing showing slightly. Sketch a squarish shape for the right front foot and a bump for the closer side of the pelvis.

By the time the average frog tadpole is three weeks old, it has developed a mouth, lost outside gills and developed inside gills, and has grown a powerful tail. By three months, its front legs appear, its scraping tadpole mouth has lost its "teeth" and is growing into a frog's wide mouth, its hind legs are growing stronger, and its tail is shorter.

⑤ Draw the toes on the front feet (including two toes that show behind the shoulder), add the mouth, and smooth the joint of the far eye. Add the crease on the left rear leg, and smooth the joints on the other legs. Erase unneeded lines.

At the end of four months, the frog's tail is almost all reabsorbed into its body, and its lungs allow it to go onto the land. It has changed from a plant-eating, water-living form to a four-legged carnivore. Three more seasons will pass before it is able to fertilize or lay eggs.

⑥ Frogs are usually green or brown with darker blotches or stripes and lighter undersides. Darken the nostril, ear, and eye, and leave white highlights and a light rim around the eyelid. Shade the lower sides of the body and limbs, and using the side of your pencil, make smudged leopard spots.

The color of the bullfrog can be olive green with dark brown spots. However, it can change to smooth pale yellow-green on a sunny day, or a nearly even dark brown if it has been in the depths of a shady pond.

MORE SCIENCE: The American bullfrog makes several sounds besides the mating call, such as the sound that tells all nearby that this is the singing frog's territory. Most startlingly, a frog in serious danger will open its mouth wide and give a sound so much like a woman's scream that humans nearby have been fooled.

The Green Sea Turtle is hunted by people for its meat and eggs. This endangered warm water turtle swims from its feeding

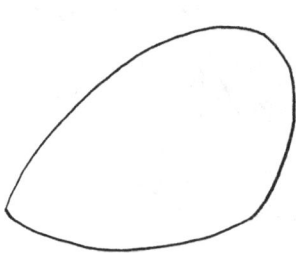

① Start with a broad almond shape for the shell with a blunt point at the left.

Sea turtles must breathe at the surface, but an adult green turtle can slow down its heartbeat to once every four to five minutes and can survive up to five hours underwater.

② Float a small, squarish shape opposite the rounded end of the shell, and draw a curved line swept back like wings.

This graceful swimmer feeds in shallow waters around tropical islands, grazing on undersea grasses. The only oceangoing turtle to bask in the sun, it will sleep on the bottom in shallow waters or on a ledge above the water level.

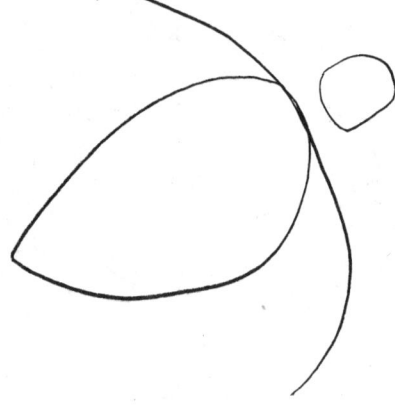

③ Make a pointed tail, and add a small, pointed shape for the far foot and a leaf shape for the near foot. Complete the forward flippers, then connect them to the head.

A nesting beach is one of any number of tropical beaches where female turtles lay their eggs, and some female turtles have been known to return to the same nesting beach for 20 years. After dark, each one may climb up the beach for 20 minutes, then take an hour to scrape out a dish-shaped pit in the sand, an egg cavity where she lays over 100 eggs. By the time she covers the eggs and hides her digging place, she may have spent four hours. During the laying season, she may make eight nests on different nights with a total of over 1,000 eggs.

grounds to dig its nest, which is nearly as far as the distance across the United States!

④ Draw in the eye and the downturned beak. Add a straight line from the top of the neck to the lower edge of the left foot. This will be the guideline for the shell pattern. Make a border for the shell that follows the outer edge on the right side. Connect the hind foot to the lower edge of the shell.

When the hatchlings are ready to escape the nest, they must wait until dark. They would die in the hot sun, and the light would make them easy prey for seabirds. The group digs out together, then the little turtles, smaller than potato chips, flop and skitter down the beach to the water.

⑤ Draw in the shell pattern, like large, interlocking leaf shapes. Use the guideline for the upper tips of the biggest sections. Be sure to make their sides curving to show the roundness of the shell. Divide the border of the shell into small segments. Wrap some lines for the wrinkles around the turtle's neck. Erase unneeded lines around the flippers and feet.

As long as a card table, this turtle's shell can be olive green to brown. The name green *refers to the color of the animal's body fat.*

⑥ Erase the center guideline. Finish the texture of the head and flipper skin with wavy lines that wrap around the shapes and cross to form an irregular network. Detail the tail, and add lines as shown around the edges of all the shell segments. Use the side of your pencil to shade the underside of the neck and jaw, as well as the flippers and tail, where they disappear beneath the shell. Darken the eye, and add the nostril.

As this turtle swims underwater, it cuts the sea grasses with an irregular sharp edge on its lower jaw. The upper beak continues to grow throughout the turtle's life.

The Northern Fence Lizard is approximately 3 inches (7.6 centimeters) long, with large ridged scales

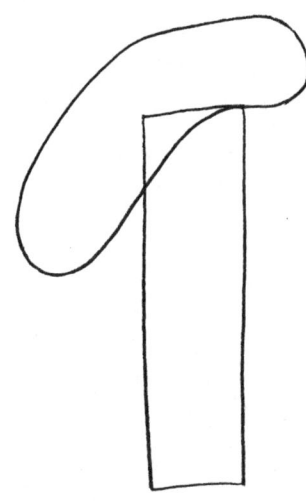

① Begin with a rectangle, which will be the post this lizard has crawled on. Add a bent tube shape at the top of the post.

This lizard is common from central Texas and Kansas east to the northeastern seaboard. It lives on snails, millipedes, spiders, and insects.

② Overlap a diamond on the tube for its head, and draw the long, curved line of the topside of the tail. Add the upper portions of the legs.

When approached slowly, this lizard will hurry away on its branch or fence rail a short distance, then disappear to the other side. But, unless followed, it may soon peek out as if playing a game of hide-and-seek. If pursued, it would rather hide than run.

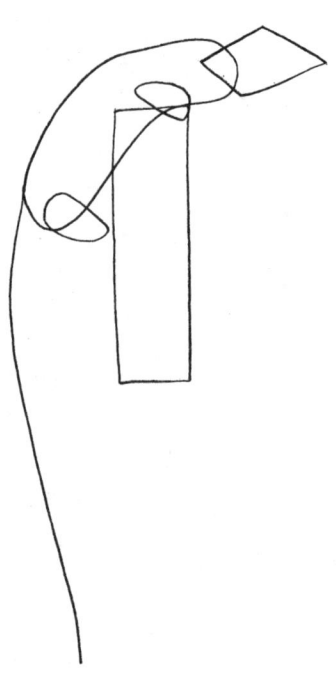

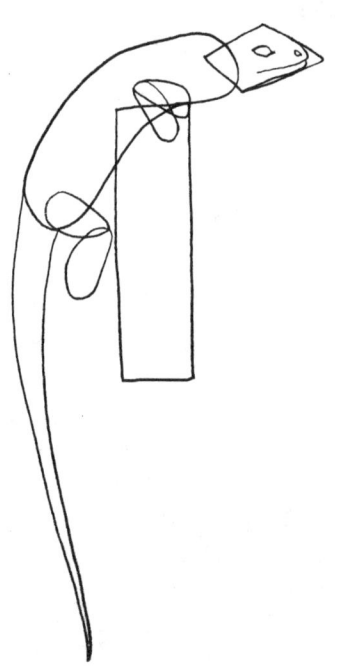

③ Continue the legs, overlapping the second joint on the first. Complete the tail outline, making it a smooth, tapering shape. Add the eye, mouth, nostril, and curving shape of the snout.

Unlike snakes, lizards' jaws are hinged behind the eyes only. The two sides of both jaws are fused at the center, so larger prey must be chewed first into small pieces before being swallowed. They have teeth for this, as well as a special sharp "egg tooth" that projects forward from the upper jaw. When hatching, babies will use it to pierce their shells.

on its back that end in dull points. It is found most often in open woods and gardens.

---

④ Draw the rounded guidelines for the toes, including a smaller loop for the front toes on the far side of the post. Smooth the connection of the head and neck above and below the chin.

This lizard hunts by rushing its victim, then crushing it in its jaws, chewing, and swallowing it.

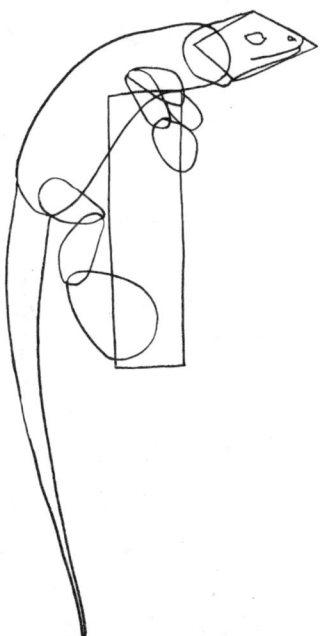

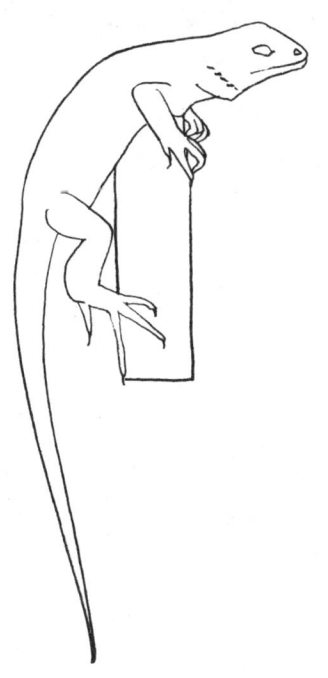

⑤ Create the spidery toes, tapering toward the tips, and add the claws. Render the crest of the head, and smooth the neck to the body. Erase unnecessary lines.

The northern fence lizard is easily identified by dark patches of intense green or blue at the base of its neck and in a stripe along its side.

⑥ Now for the detail work! Add the texture of the spiny skin with dark, backward-pointing thorns along the lizard's back and short, wavy markings on its back, neck, legs, and head. Use light crossed lines to indicate the pattern of the scales under the tail and on the back and legs. Short, heavy strokes will give the texture of the rough scales. Darken the nostril and the eye, leaving white specks for shine on the eyeball. Add a small additional piece of wood to the post, and if you wish, finish the fence post with a wavy light-and-dark wood grain.

There are over 3,500 different species of lizards that live around the world. Almost one-third of these species descend from the skink family.

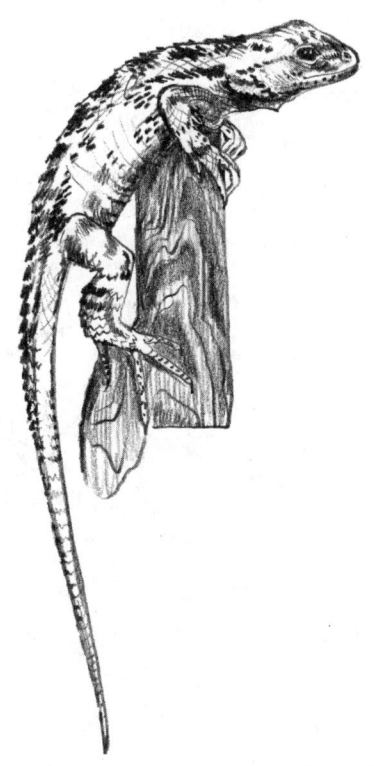

47

The American Alligator is one of the oldest species on earth and has survived in Florida

① Draw two long, flattened ovals touching at the ends, one on its side, the other tilted up slightly.

Crocodilians (alligators are part of this group) are the most advanced of all reptiles and have an internal body and brain structure, including a heart similar to a human's. A male American alligator is considered large at 13 feet (4 meters) long.

② Make a narrow loop from the left end of the flat oval, which will be the tail's upper edge. Draw egg shapes for the visible upper legs and a slightly curved box for the open jaw area. Notice that the box is about half the length of the tilted oval it overlaps.

You can tell an alligator from a crocodile by the alligator's broad snout and head, and its teeth, which don't show when the mouth is closed.

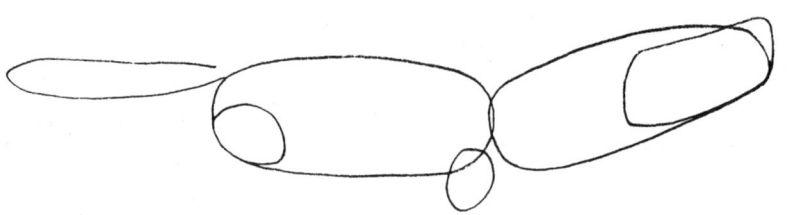

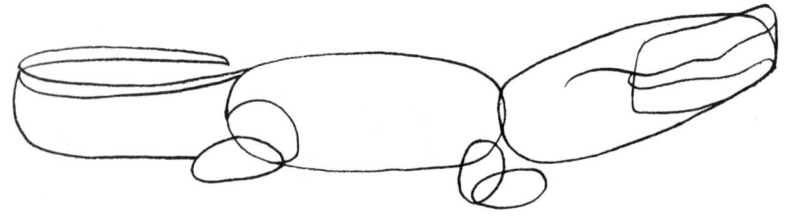

③ Draw in the lower edge of the tail. Make a second upper-edge line that echoes the shape of the first loop. Add ovals for the lower legs. Starting at the top right corner of the jaw box, bring a slightly wavy line backward nearly to the other end of the oval. Outline the upper edge of the lower jaw, creating the open mouth.

The tail, which is taller than it is broad, is used for swimming. When the animal bursts from shallow water to attack wading deer or wild pigs, the powerful tail knocks down a victim or breaks its leg before the alligator seizes it between its jaws.

for 57 million years. Man has only been on earth in his present form for 200,000 years.

---

④ Draw in the eye, forehead crest, and bumpy head connecting to the body shape. Add ovals for the feet, and make lines along the back for the rows of osteoderms (squarish, thickened skin plates that protect the back).

Surprisingly, both American and Chinese alligators, which are thought of as tropical animals, can survive in water in freezing weather. The body lies in deeper, warmer water, while the nose pokes through a hole in the ice. Internal body temperatures of 41° Fahrenheit (5° Celsius) have been recorded, and the animals have recovered completely.

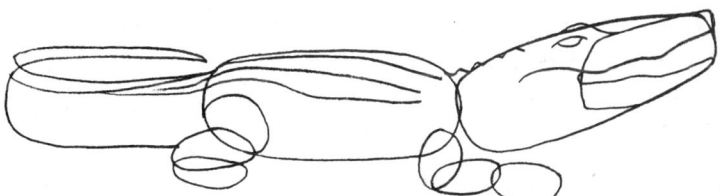

⑤ Smooth the leg joints, and draw in the toes and claws. Add the round eyeball. Draw vertical lines on the tail, which are divisions between rows of thickened squares of skin. Create scallop-shaped fins called scutes on the upper edges of the tail to eventually form one row at the tail's end. Draw these angled slightly backward toward the tail. Erase unneeded lines.

Through the ages, some crocodilian relatives have developed thicker back armor, while some creatures' skin has thinned. Scientists believe that, in addition to protection, these large bony plates, or scutes, help the animals regulate their body temperature by bringing blood to the surface for warming or cooling.

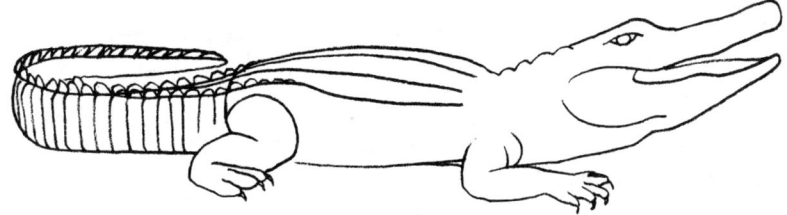

⑥ Finish the alligator with shallow, shaded oval bumps on the back. Draw the divisions of the back armor, crossing the horizontal lines. The thinner skin wrinkles on the sides and neck can be made with a screen of lines that curve around the body. Using short, dark strokes, highlight the scales on the head, legs, and tail. Shade the tail scutes and the undersides of all the limbs. Make the pointed teeth almost all the same size and curving slightly backward. Darken the eye and inside of the mouth.

The American alligator has been known to eat small calves, and very occasionally, people, but the usual diet in its first year of life is insects, then snakes, turtles, snails, slow-moving fish, and small mammals and birds.

MORE SCIENCE: It is estimated that only two out of 100 alligator hatchlings survive to become an adult.

The Ornate Box Turtle

like all turtles, is part of the reptile class. It is the first animal with a backbone whose

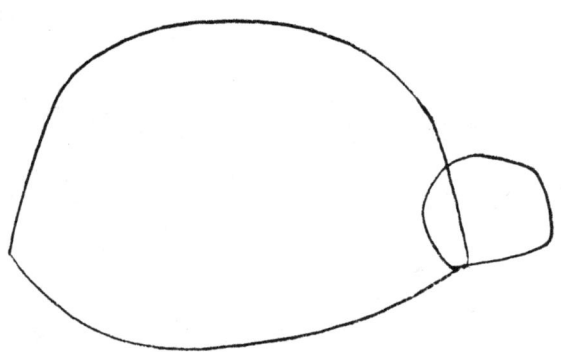

① Make the tall dome of the shell, its lower edge curved. Overlap a smaller dome for the head.

When full grown, this turtle will fit easily within the rim of a small saucer (4 to 5¾ inches—10 to 14.6 centimeters—long). However, it may live for 50 years, and some older than 100 years have been recorded.

② Draw in the eye, and add an oval for the upper front leg and a club shape for the hind leg. Within the original dome, continue the curve of the shell's upper edge, creating an almond shape that will become the top of the upper shell, called a carapace.

This species is common in the central United States and lives in dry areas like prairies and open woods. It helps humans by eating insects that damage crops like grasshoppers, caterpillars, and scavenger beetles.

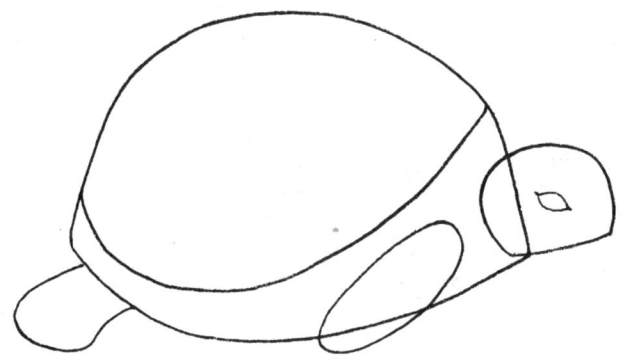

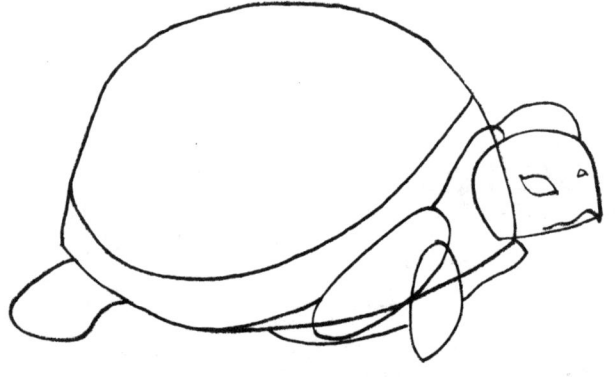

③ Draw a vertical oval for the front foot and a partial oval for the foot that shows behind the head. Now draw the curved edge of the lower shell, which disappears beneath the turtle's chin. Add the edge of the upper shell that curves up from the belly, disappears behind the front leg, and curves up over the head. Add the nostril and beak.

A turtle has two hard shells—one on top and one underneath. The shells protect the body from drying out in the sun and from getting too hot or too cold. When an animal such as a dog, coyote, crow, or hawk tries to grab the turtle's leg or pick at its head to kill it, this turtle can pull in its head and legs and tightly close the front of its lower shell, which acts like a door on a hinge.

body allowed it to live and lay eggs on dry land. Though they are well-adapted to life on earth today, a number of species are in danger of being wiped out by human hunters and people moving into their territories.

④ Draw in the claws on the hind foot and the triangle at the hind edge of the shell, which is its flaring edge. Sketch in the sections, or scutes, of this turtle's shell, which fit together like puzzle pieces.

The turtle's shell has two main layers—it is formed by bones that interlock, similar to your skull bones. Over the bones are plates of thickened skin, like the scales on any reptile. You can tell if the turtle is growing because as it grows, a new layer forms under the scales, and you will see a ridge around each one that is lighter in color than the rest of the shell.

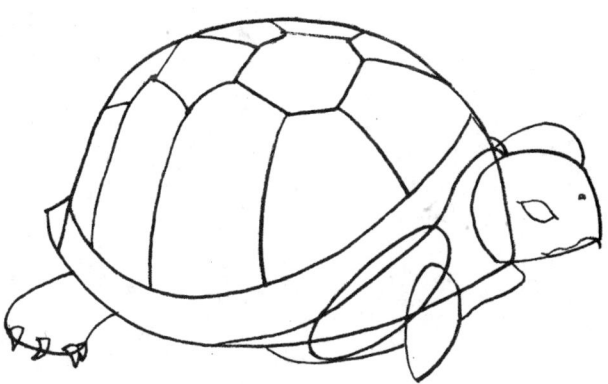

⑤ Draw the dividing lines between each section of the shell's border, and add the claws on the front foot. Finish the edge of the lower shell that shows between the front and hind leg. Make the head more boxy shaped as shown, and erase unneeded lines.

This turtle finds a mate in spring and buries two to eight eggs, which hatch in about two months. The baby turtles, just over 1 inch (2.5 centimeters) long, hatch by themselves and are on their own to find insects, caterpillars, and berries for food.

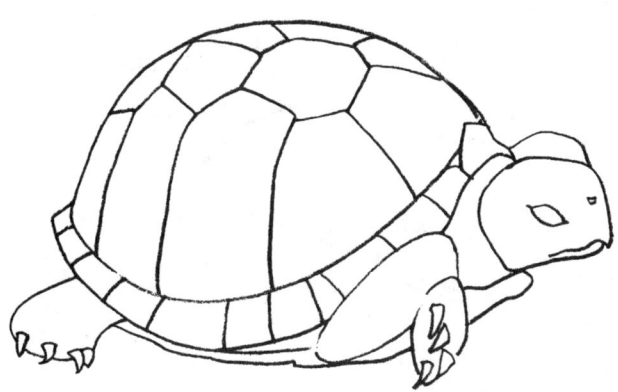

⑥ The shell is dark with pale yellow or cream-colored bars. Leave the bars unshaded, and darken the rest of the shell around them. Darken the dividing lines where the scutes of the shell meet, as well as the lines within the border scutes. The legs and feet have thick, wrinkled skin, and on the front foot are larger scales. The head is dark with yellowish spots, and the neck is wrinkled. Darken below the edge of the shell, the lower edges of the head and legs, the claws, and the eye, leaving a white highlight.

On mornings from April to October, you may see this turtle lying in a sunny spot until it is warm enough to hunt for food. In the summer, it may cool itself in a pond. In cold weather, it digs a burrow to hibernate.

The Tuatara
lives on small islands in the South Pacific off the coast of New Zealand. It looks like a lizard, but it is special because it is the only animal alive from a group of

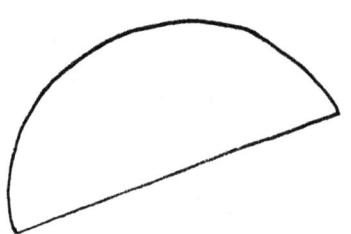

① Draw a half-circle at a slight angle.

The name tuatara *is a native New Zealand word meaning "peaks on the back." Millions of years ago relatives of this reptile lived in many parts of the world, including North and South America and Europe.*

② Add a flat-sided pear shape for the head, about half as long as the body shape. Sketch the visible upper legs.

One reason these animals have avoided extinction may be because they can function at much lower temperatures than other ectotherms (animals that depend on the temperature of their surroundings). A tuatara can feed and move quickly at between 43° and 61° Fahrenheit (6° and 16° Celsius). They also live a long time, up to 120 years.

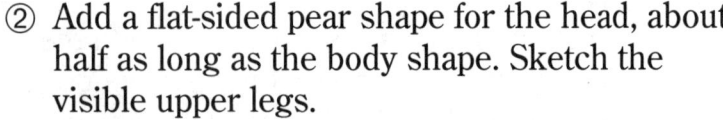

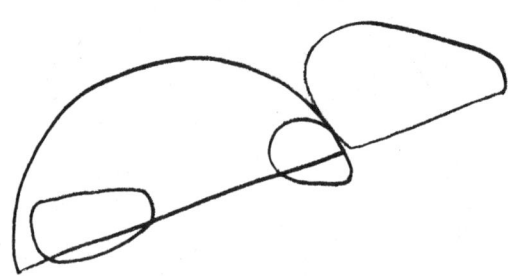

③ Connect the upper edge of the head to the body, and draw a long curving line from the back to form the top of the tail. Add the lower hind leg oval.

This 1- to 2-foot-long (30 to 61 centimeters) reptile stays near the nesting places of seabirds whose waste attracts ground insects like the beetles the tuatara eats. They also feed on spiders, earthworms, slugs, snails, and sometimes the chicks of seabirds.

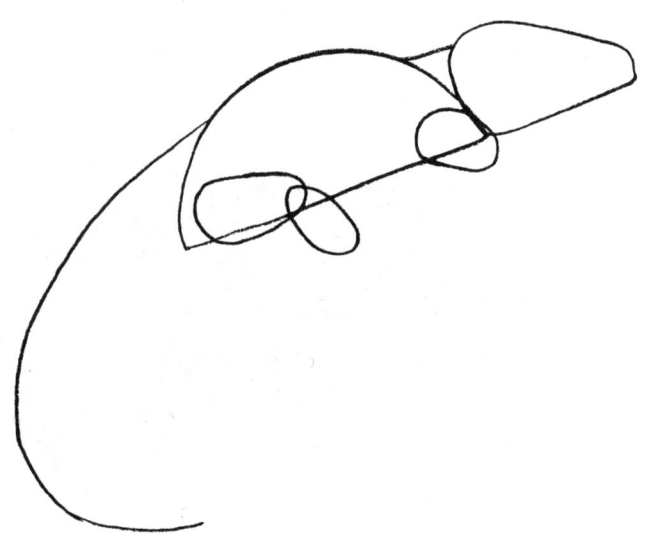

reptiles that lived before the dinosaurs. When you look at a tuatara, you can see what some animals were like 220 million years ago!

④ Complete the broad, tapering tail, and add the outlines for the feet. Make the eye large and the mouth curved up slightly at the corner.

One unusual feature of this shy reptile is a third "eye" on top of its head. This eye has a lens, a light-sensitive surface, and is connected to the brain. It cannot, however, see images.

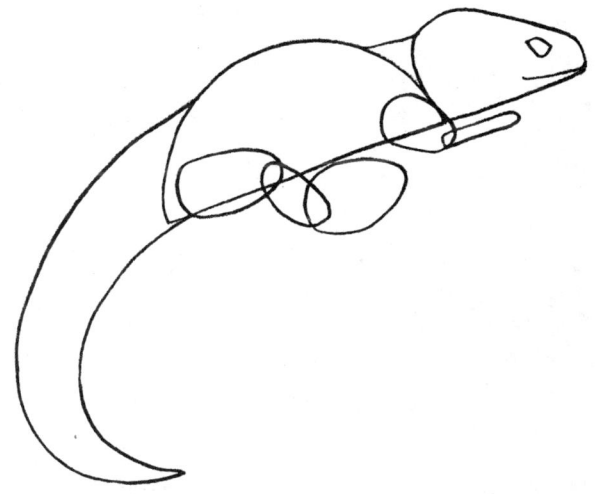

⑤ Refine the head shape with the ridge of the farther eye, and sketch in wrinkles along the jaw line. Draw in toes, claws, and spines along the back and tail. Smooth connections, and erase unnecessary lines.

The eyes of the tuatara are specially adapted for its activity at night as well as during the day, like those of crocodiles and turtles. They may have evolved from a time when the eyes were used to help the animal regulate its active and sleeping times.

⑥ Shade the spines so they look rounded, and draw in skin wrinkles. Using short, curved lines, shade in the toes, and the lower side of the tail, head, and body. If you want to color it, use an olive green for the back, and a light tan or white for the spines, lower jaw, and belly. The upper body is spotted in the lighter color. Provide a rock for the tuatara to bask on, and make it look round by shading under the animal's body.

Probably the reason the tuatara has lasted so long when its relatives died out everywhere else is because the New Zealand area became separated by sea from other land masses where predators lived. Now the animal is in danger from disturbances by humans, and the New Zealand Wildlife Act has made killing or collecting the tuatara a crime in order to protect its future.

The Western Diamondback Rattlesnake

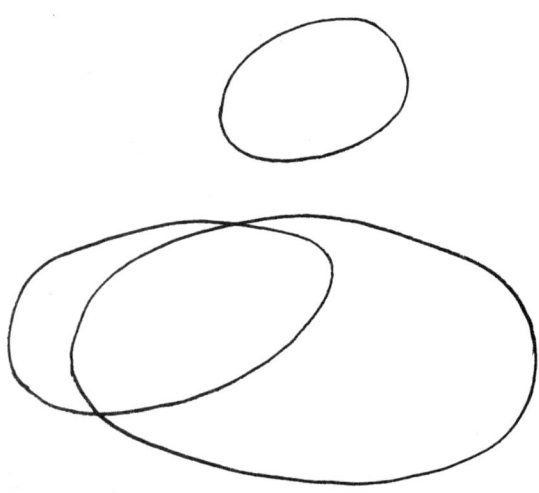

① This western diamondback is coiled and threatening its prey before it strikes. Start with three ovals, the largest at the bottom of your drawing area, the next overlapping at an angle, and the third hanging above the center of the bottom one.

Most rattlers feed almost entirely on warm-blooded animals that they hunt at night. Using the sense organs in their tongue, they can "smell" a mouse or ground squirrel. When they strike, they pump venom into the victim through one or both of the curved fangs that fold down from the top of the mouth.

② Begin to render the two bottom ovals into donut shapes with lines that follow the curve of the ovals' lower edges. Then use lines to connect the upper oval to the larger one.

There is reason to stay a safe distance from a rattlesnake. Its venom acts on the blood and circulatory system of any animal, including humans, and if not treated with antitoxin, death can occur. Among poisonous snakes, the rattler's venom is very strong, and the average amount of venom in a western diamondback is enough to kill 4,000 mice!

③ Complete the donut hole for the largest oval. Add the small egg shape for the head and the tube shape of the tail, which holds the snake's rattles.

The rattle is a series of hornlike shells that grows an additional section each time the snake sheds its skin. However, the age of the snake can't be told by the number of rattles. Some may be broken off by wear and tear, and a young snake may shed up to seven times in its first year, while an older one may shed only once or twice a year.

has measured as large as just under 8 feet (2.5 meters) long, while the average length for a rattlesnake is 4 to 5 feet (1.2 to 1.5 meters). With 30 species of rattlesnakes, the two largest are the western and eastern diamondback.

④ Connect the head oval with its upper body loop using a curving pair of lines. Then, on the lower two ovals, add two lines, one on the lower for the back ridge, and one on the upper for the joint between the side scales and the belly scales. Above the head oval, draw the ridge for the farther eye and the tip of the snout. Draw the eye, mouth, nostril, and a second nostril-type opening—a pit—near the mouth.

The pit is a forward-facing opening through which the snake senses the heat given off by a warm-blooded animal, either prey or predator. From the heat, the snake can tell how close it is to the creature.

⑤ Go over the whole length of the snake's body, and make sure each loop is smooth and even. Refine the tip of its tail, then carefully erase the extra lines.

The distinguishing characteristic of this kind of snake is the rattle at the end of its tail, which is made of keratin, the same material that forms animal claws and human fingernails.

⑥ Draw crisscrossed lines that form a network wrapping around the snake's body. These are guidelines for the scales. Use light pencil strokes for these lines. Detail the eye, and add vertical lines behind it. On the snake's rattler, sketch in wavy horizontal lines.

A snake's body is almost completely covered with small areas of thick scales. The scales protect the skin from scratches and give it a coloring that blends with its surroundings. While a particular species of rattler can be described as having a certain pattern, the colors in the pattern can vary, depending on the colors of the soil and plants where it lives.

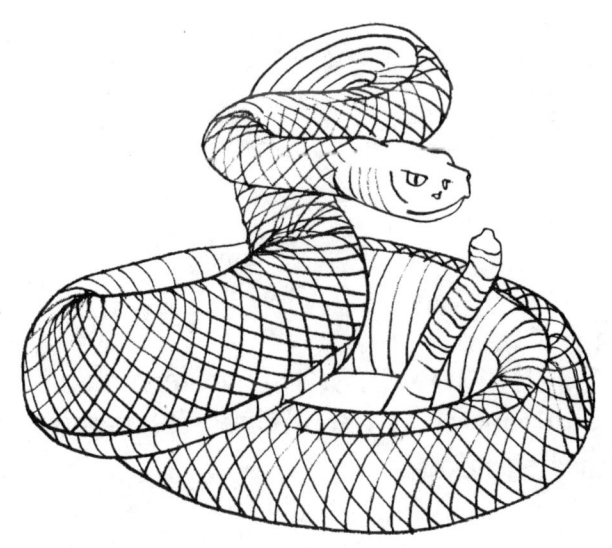

⑦ Put in the scale patterns. Note that the scales on the head are irregular and form a rim around the jaws and eye. In the center of the upper jaw, the scale has a notch for the tongue. Detail the lines wrapping around the tip of the tail to show the rattles. The rattle section is rather wide and flat. The tail tip on this species has several black-and-white stripes just before the rattles. Finally, add shading, making sure the lower edge of each coil is shaded, and the coils nearer the back are darker than those in front.

The snake's tongue "tastes" the air to identify either prey or predator. Its eyesight is not very strong, but between its sense of smell and heat-sensing pit, it can strike very accurately for over one-half its full length and at 6 to 10 feet (1.8 to 3 meters) per second. Sometimes it moves with such violence, the entire body leaves the ground!

MORE SCIENCE: The western diamondback is the most common venomous snake in the southwestern United States. It has most likely caused the death of more people than any other snake in the region.

Backgrounds

Once you have completed a drawing, you may want to put your reptile or amphibian in a setting. These creatures live in a variety of different settings, but you can add all sorts of things to make the scenery unusual and interesting. Nature magazines or books on reptiles and amphibians will show you environments in which these animals live. Or, use your imagination! Here are some suggestions for creating different settings.

MAGAZINE BACKGROUNDS

If you like to cut and paste, ask your family for some old magazines you can cut up. You can make a crazy collage by finding pictures of various sizes to add to the composition. Try to cut them out so as little of their original background shows as possible.

Glue sticks are a tidy way to apply adhesive. Place the cutout facedown on a piece of scrap paper. If you hold the cutout with one finger and stroke outward from the center with the glue stick, you'll have the best chance of spreading the glue evenly and not tearing or ruffling up the paper's edges.

PAINTED BACKGROUNDS

You don't need a paintbrush to add these painted backgrounds! To create a ground texture, use an old sponge, crumpled paper (like paper towels), or even the pattern on the fingertips of rubber gloves. Dip the material lightly in some paint you have spread in a jar lid, and print the pattern, overlapping until you have the darkness and texture you want. Practice on scrap paper until you have an idea of how it will look. If your drawing is large enough, you can use this painting method to make a texture on the reptile or amphibian itself. Be sure to leave space around the edges of your creature, or it will disappear in the pattern!

TEXTURED BACKGROUNDS

If you want to create a textured background, first draw your animal on a thin piece of paper. Place a textured object (such as sandpaper) under the section of your paper where you want the texture to appear. Now grab a pencil with a soft lead. Then, using the side of the pencil lead, rub lightly and evenly over the area. To create a wood pattern, use rough-surfaced wood (unpainted works best). You can use anything from the side of a key to paper clips. Move the paper slightly so the textures of the objects overlap for interesting effects. Again, be sure to leave space around your creature so that it doesn't disappear in your rubbed texture.

SHADOWED BACKGROUNDS

By adding shadows in the right places, your animals will leap off the page! Imagine where the shadow of your reptile or amphibian would fall underneath the body, legs, and tail. Then fill in those areas with a dark pencil. You can copy pictures of plants or rocky areas for realistic backgrounds—keeping the animal the lightest part of the drawing—or you can make up a setting. Work carefully, making sure you fill in every area you want dark. Also shade up to the edge of the reptile or amphibian. Remember to draw the shadows touching the animal's feet where they meet the surface.

Bringing Your Animal to Life

Here are more tips on how to put life into your drawings. Keep in mind that the most realistic drawings combine several finishing techniques. You can practice and experiment with your own favorite combinations!

CONTOUR DRAWING

Even if you don't plan to fill in your drawing with color or texture, you can make your animal look more solid by changing the darkness and width of its outlines. For example, note the difference in the line weight within the drawing of the giant land tortoise. The lower edges of the shell are thicker to suggest shadows. Also, whenever a line bends or meets another line, it thickens. This technique not only makes the animal's shape appear more three-dimensional, but it also makes the drawing more fun to look at.

CASTING SHADOWS

The simplest thing you can do to make your drawing look rounded and real is to give it a shadow. To do this, you must imagine where the shadow of its form would be if light was coming from above the reptile or amphibian. The warty newt casts a shadow directly underneath its body because the light source is directly above it. Notice that the underside of the body is all in shadow.

LIGHT FIGURE, DARK BACKGROUND

You'll be surprised by how rounded your reptile or amphibian looks if you simply darken the space behind it. By darkening the space behind this green sea turtle, you can create a rounded, three-dimensional effect. You can imagine looking into a dark ocean and seeing this turtle swimming to shore. Placing shading on the turtle itself adds to the rounded look, as well as the effect of being in the space rather than on top of a flat black shape.

Making Your Animal Seem Larger (or Smaller)

How do you make an animal in a small drawing seem larger? Or an animal in a huge picture seem smaller? The following techniques will show you how.

THE HORIZON LINE

To show how big your creature is in a drawing, add a ground line or horizon line across your picture. If your reptile or amphibian is very small, you can make it appear larger by drawing it inside a matchbox. This would place the horizon line where the side of the box meets the floor. Normally, the horizon line is on the viewer's eye level. So, if the top of the animal's body is drawn higher than the horizon line, it seems larger. If the horizon is near the top of your picture and the creature is toward the bottom, it seems smaller. This Komodo dragon appears to be gigantic as it towers over the trees and the small river.

REALISTIC SCALE

If a person has never seen a Jackson's chameleon, it is hard for him or her to know exactly how big one is. So, if you draw the lizard as it might actually be, on a plant whose size most people know, you can convey an accurate measurement of this creature.

Tips on Color

Your picture will stand out from the rest of the crowd if you use these helpful tips on how to add color to your masterpiece!

TRY WHITE ON BLACK

For a different look, try working on black construction paper or art paper. Then, instead of pencil, use white chalk, white prismacolor pencil, or poster paint. With this technique, you'll need to concentrate on drawing the light areas in your picture rather than the dark ones. Your dramatic Indopacific crocodile is even more stunning when put against a black background!

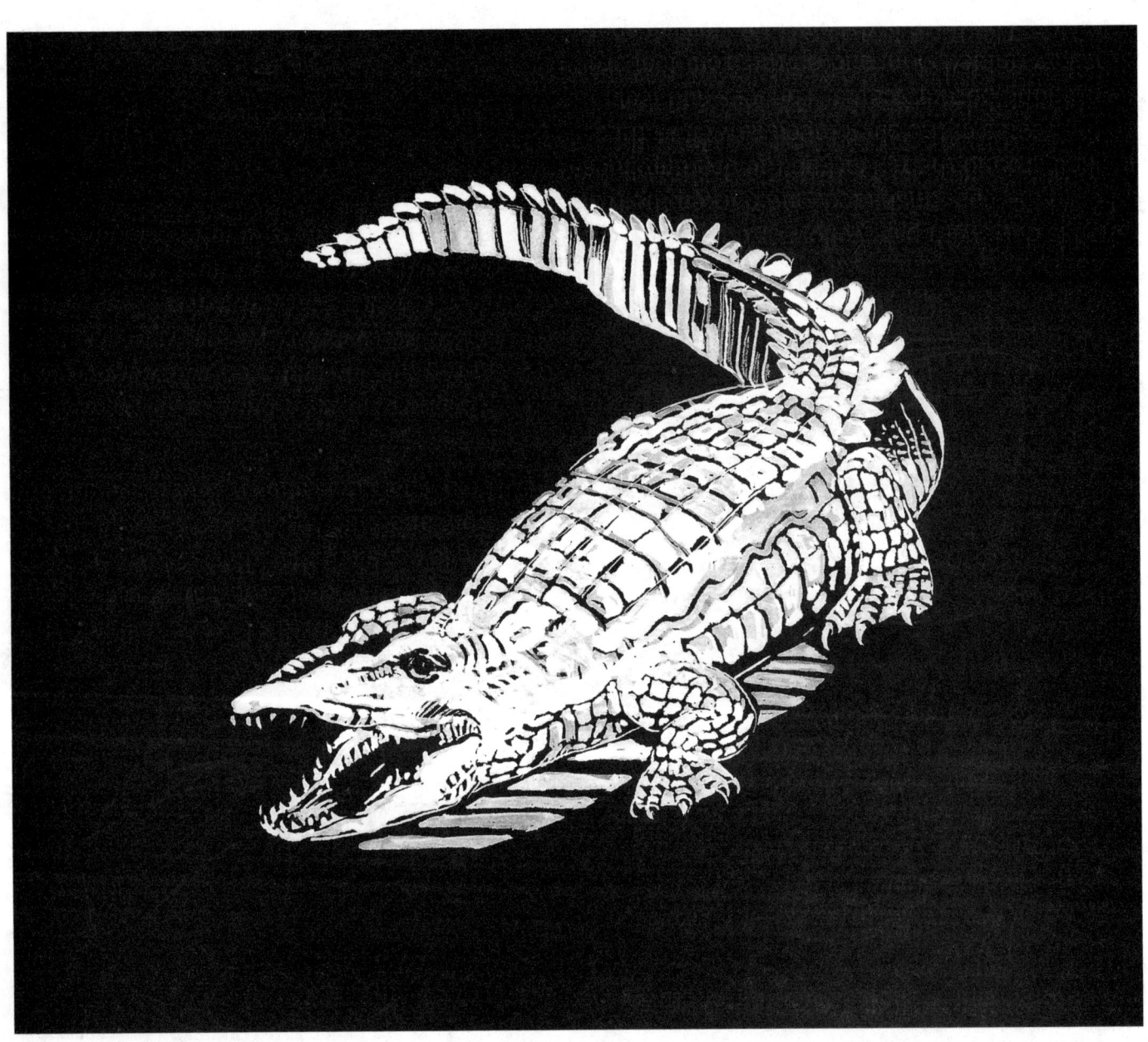

TRY BLACK AND WHITE ON GRAY (OR TAN)

You don't need special gray or tan paper from the art store for this technique. Instead, try cutting apart the inside of a grocery bag or a cereal box. This time, your background is a middle tone (neither light nor dark). Sketch your reptile or amphibian in black, then use white to make highlights. Add black for the shadows. Don't completely cover up the tan or gray of the cardboard. Let it be the middle tone within your illustration. With this technique, your pictures can have a very finished look with a minimal amount of drawing, such as in the picture below of the Gulf Coast toad.

TRY COLOR

Instead of using every color in your marker set or your colored pencil set, try drawing in black for shadows, white for highlights, and one color for a middle tone. This third color blended with the white creates a fourth color. You will be surprised how professional your drawing will look.

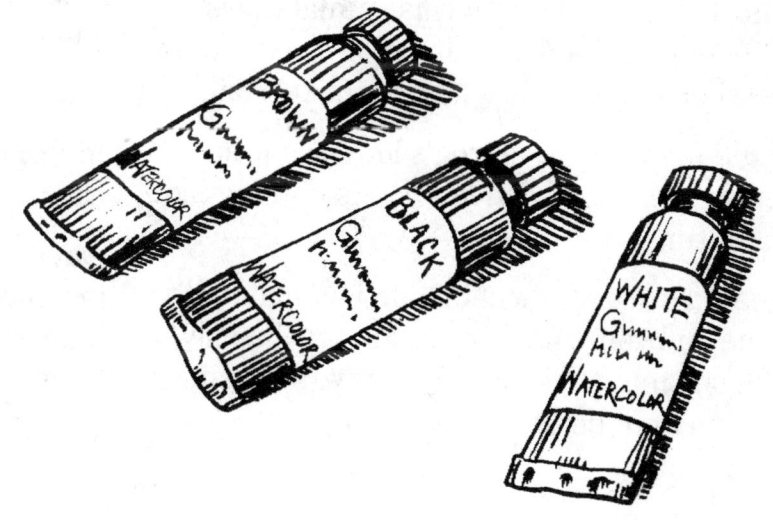

Glossary

amphibian: a class of cold-blooded, backboned animals characterized by their ability to live both on land and in water. Usually, amphibian babies first live in water, then mature into air-breathing adults and live on land.

burrow: a hole in the ground used for shelter, such as that used by the giant land tortoise

carapace: a bony shell covering the back of an animal, as in a turtle

cold-blooded: a characteristic of reptiles, in which their body temperature is dependent on their surroundings

crocodilian: a group of reptiles, including crocodiles and alligators and their extinct ancestors

ectotherm: a cold-blooded animal

evolution: the gradual change of animal groups over years and years

gills: the parts of many water animals that make it possible to breathe in water

habitat: the place or environment where a plant or animal lives under natural conditions

hibernate: to rest or be in a sleeplike state

keratin: the material that forms animal claws and human fingernails and hair. It makes up the rattle at the end of a diamondback rattlesnake's tail.

larva: the first stage of a frog's life once it has hatched from its shell, when it looks nothing like its adult form

mammal: a class of warm-blooded animals with a backbone and some hair or fur. Rather than lay eggs, female mammals usually carry their babies inside them until birth.

osteoderm: a squarish, thickened skin plate that protects the back of the American alligator and other reptiles

pit: a forward-facing opening through which a snake senses heat given off by a warm-blooded animal, either prey or predator

polliwog: a tadpole

predator: a hunter; a creature that hunts other creatures for food

prey: the victim of a hunter

reptile: a cold-blooded, backboned animal with scaly skin. Most reptiles have four legs and three to five clawed toes. The snake is a reptile that doesn't have legs.

scales: small hard, thin plates that cover the bodies of many animals

scavenge: to eat the remains of dead animals. The Komodo dragon is a scavenger.

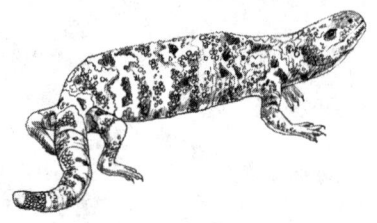

scutes: protective bony plates or fins found on some reptiles, such as the ornate box turtle

spermatophore: a packet or mass of reproducing material carried by the male to the female in some animals

tadpole: a baby frog, also called a polliwog

toxin: a poison naturally made by some animals, usually used in defense

warm-blooded: a characteristic of some animals, in which their body temperature is regulated internally and is not dependent on the outside temperature or climate